BLISS

BLISS

Managing Mayhem

By
R.E.S. TIDMORE

Ruthless Writers
Publishing & Design

Bliss: Book 1 (Managing Mayhem Series)
Copyright © 2014 R.E.S. Tidmore
All rights reserved

Ruthless Writers Publishing & Design

Fifth Edition

Printed ISBN: 978-0989524346
Ebook ISBN: 978-0989524339

Cover Design by Ruth Spickelmire
Book formatting by R. W. Publishing & Design

Other Titles

The Awakener Series
Awaken
Oblivion
Torn

The Verbecks of Idaho
Midnight's Dream
Delicate Dream
Unbroken Dream

Managing Mayhem
Bliss

Coming Soon
D is for Defective

Dedication

To all the heroes who serve.
Thank You

CHAPTER ONE

The doorbell chimed, jolting River in her chair. Who the heck could it be at nine in the morning? It was Tuesday, and Joe from the grocery store only delivered on Wednesdays. She pushed down the lump that formed in her throat at the prospect of an unknown human interaction at her door. *I will not cower, but overcome,* she told herself, trying not to feel too silly about the new mantra her therapist instructed she use when her anxiety surfaced. Maybe whoever it was would leave.

She leaned back in her chair, which let out a protesting groan, and stared at the manuscript of her favorite client, author A.J. Wrath. Something was missing from the story, and though her brain searched for the missing piece, the damn thing kept dancing out of her reach. Three piles of manuscripts awaited her attention, but she needed to figure out the Wrath storyline first. Being an editor of a small publishing house kept her busier than she'd anticipated. She took the job six years ago after graduating from college. She hadn't left the house in weeks for anything other than a solitary jog, and she hadn't taken a vacation in years.

She gazed out the window of her second-story office. The backyard really needed some TLC. The tall grass needed to be mowed. Her peach tree—lush with bright green leaves and heavy with fruit—needed to be picked. The corners of her mouth pulled into a smile when she spotted the top of a ladder next to the wooden fence poking out from her neighbor's side of the yard.

Her elderly neighbor loved River's peaches. Last year, River spied her on a ladder pulling a branch over to her side of the fence with a long hook. Her face was one of pure delight and impish guilt for her thievery. River didn't mind. She enjoyed watching the shenanigans from her window.

Three knocks—heavy and hard—pounded on her door. River froze. Another three knocks. What did they want? Her mind came up with all different scenarios: There was a shooter on the loose in the neighborhood. There was a gas leak and she would need to evacuate. Someone blew a tire and wanted to use my phone because theirs was died . . . *Come on, get it together.*

In stockinged feet, she carefully avoided the squeaky wooden boards that would give away her presence on the staircase. Stopping on a middle step, she bent low to peer out the small glass window in the center of the front door. No one could see her. She'd done a triple check with her older brother, Mathew, before buying this house three years ago. He'd thought it was foolish that she worried about such things, but she'd never told him about being assaulted one night in college by a lost drunk from a football game. To this day, her worry meter kicked up a notch with strangers. It was one of the main reasons she'd taken the editor position because she could work from home.

She and Mathew shared two years at Boise State University together. He was a part-time student because he liked working more than being in class. She, however, had gotten an academic scholarship as well as a spot on the track team, so she was a full-timer. It was the best two years in her college experience. They went everywhere together, parties, football games, even took a few elective classes together. When Mathew dropped out to join the Marines, the world closed in on her. There was no way she would tell him about what had happened that night. It was a weight he didn't have to bear. She loved him too much to make him worry about her when he had to focus on his own life overseas.

She crept down another step and a deafening scream tore through her mind at the sight of two marines in dress uniform standing on her porch. She bolted downstairs, fumbled with the lock on the door, then wrenched it open. The two men jumped at her sudden appearance.

"Mathew . . . is he okay?"

"Hello, ma'am," said the marine with the blue eyes. "Are you River Connelly?"

"Yes," she said, clutching the door, too afraid her knees would give out.

"May we come inside?" the other marine asked with a grim look on his face.

There were two reasons marines came knocking on doors: Mathew was hurt, or Mathew was . . . no. No, please . . .

She recalled the date and counted the days. The last time she'd spoken to Mathew was over three weeks ago. It wasn't uncommon for them to go a week or so without talking, but three? How had she not noticed that?

"There's no point." Her eyes burned with tears. "Tell me. I can handle it."

"As you wish, ma'am. I'm sorry to inform you that Mathew Wagner was killed in a car accident on July sixth. Magen Wagner was notified of the death of her son on July seventh."

What was today . . . July 14th. A week. Mathew had been dead for a week. Why had it taken so long to find out? River held back the scream that threatened to explode from her chest.

"No, please, God . . . not Mathew." Nausea hit, and she let go of the door. She gazed at the men through watery eyes, her hand covering her mouth. "I'll be fine."

The blue-eyed marine nodded, pulled out a business card, and held it out to her. "If you have any questions, please feel free to call us."

She took the card in her shaky hand and with a quick nod, she closed the door in their faces.

The world shrank. She made it two steps before collapsing to her knees. Mathew was dead. He was thirty-one and he was killed. Her Mathew was gone. A sob was torn from in between the pieces of her breaking heart. She rubbed off layers of skin from her arms as she rocked back and forth. She screamed again and again, lost in heartbreak.

"Please God, no . . . don't let it be true. Don't let him be gone. I'll do anything you ask, just don't let him be gone." She rocked harder, slamming her fist on the floor as the anger of her grief grew. She bent forward and dry heaved. Her world turning to ash around her. Time past unnoticed.

The phone rang. The noise was piercing. River managed to peel herself off the floor and cross the room. She glared at the caller ID: Megan Wagner. A wave of disappointment threatened to overtake her emotions, but she needed to pull herself together. Breathe in for three seconds, exhale for six seconds . . . a breathing technique her therapist taught her to slow her heart rate.

After hesitating, she picked up the receiver. "Hello, Mother."

A matter-a-fact voice lashed out at her. "Why haven't you called me?"

River's fingers strangled the phone. "I should be asking you the same thing."

"So you know about Mathew's death, I take it. I've been trying to reach you for days. Haven't you checked your messages? I've taken care of everything while you sat locked up in that house of yours."

River took a deep breath. Her chest tightened. The only other person in the world who could kick up her anxiety other than a stranger was her mother. *Damn it.* Her mother had called her last week, but River had ignored it. The way her mother treated her, she wondered if hearing about Mathew's death from two strangers was the better option.

"Mathew was the one person I loved in this world. I—"

"You need to stop being so crazy and leave that damn house of yours . . ."

River's jaw dropped. She pulled the phone away from her ear and gawked at it in disbelief. Deep breaths, she reminded herself.

"Whatever your mood, it's of no concern—"

River cut her off. "Yes, that would be too motherly for you, being concerned for your daughter at the death of your son and her brother. That would be asking too much." She trembled. Angry hot embers seared in her chest. She could never make her mother happy. River was either wearing the wrong clothes, had a bad haircut, or couldn't stand up straight enough for her mother. It had always been exhausting.

"Don't you talk to me that way. It's insubordination and I will not tolerate it." River's mother was a master chief in the US Navy and had little patience for confrontation.

"What do you want, Mother?" River asked. Tired and heartbroken.

"Your brother has been buried at Point Loma cemetery in California."

"What?" she shouted.

"Really, River, did you think your brother would stay fresh? He had to be buried. It's been a week since the accident."

River quickly hung up the phone. Hot tears filled her eyes, and a sob caught in her throat. Her brother was dead, and her mother had buried him eight hundred miles away. She didn't get to say good-bye. Of all things her mother had done, this was the worst.

The phone rang once more. This time she didn't move. The answering machine picked up. Her mother's voice echoed through the house.

"Well, that was rude. Just so you know, your brother put your name on all of his paperwork since he wasn't married. Everything's yours: the insurance money, the house, and the bills. Have fun with all the paperwork and packing his house up," her mother choked out. "I emailed you the report of the accident if you want to know what happen." Then a dial tone filled the air.

River yanked the cord of the phone out of the wall, and threw it across the room. The instrument exploded, fragments skidding everywhere. Her right eyelid twitched rapidly. She hated her mother. How could the woman be so cold-blooded? No wonder her father left when she was six. Didn't even bother with a divorce, just left. Poof, gone! Looking back, it was a smart move. Her mother would have made him miserable. Her mother changed their last names after he left to her maiden name. Mathew Connelly became Mathew Wagner and so did she. But when River turned eighteen, she'd changed it back to Connelly.

She collapsed onto the couch, the room spinning wildly. "Mathew . . ." she called out. Her mother's voice rang in her ears. She grabbed a pillow and screamed into it.

CHAPTER TWO

Maddox Bliss strolled into Whiskey-Tango-Foxtrot, a bar in Oceanside, California, he'd inherited from his father. For a Thursday, it was crowded.

Damn. He couldn't even walk into his own bar. As he approached people scurried out of his way. He gave them each a nod and moved through the crowd. He positioned himself behind the bar and leaned against the wall, scrutinizing the new honey-stained ceiling beams and counters. He was pleased with the bright, warm feeling the honey-stained wood gave the place. Each wall of the Whiskey-Tango-Foxtrot was dedicated to a US military branch: Navy, Marine, Army, and Air Force. All were admired and respected at WTF. Bliss had no tolerance for branch conflict in his bar, and all who entered knew that. All military fought to protect the American people and their freedoms. In the grand scheme of war, all were needed to get shit done.

Bliss puffed up, overtaken with pride. He joined the navy when he was seventeen, his father signing off to have him shipped to Great Lakes, IL for boot camp. His father had hopes of seeing his son take to a military life instead of the life of an entrepreneur. Sixteen years later, Bliss was a navy chief and a craftmaster in charge of his own hovercraft and its crew. The hovercraft unit where he was stationed was his home away from home.

Bliss sighed. It had been two weeks since Gunnery Sergeant Mathew Wagner died. He thought of Wagner often, the weight of guilt pressing down on him, and some days it felt overwhelming.

He'd missed the funeral . . . if there even was one. So he and the Mayhem Managers picked a random Thursday morning to take off from the unit and go to the gravesite to pay their respects. Bliss had regarded the gunmetal-veined tombstone with regret. He toed the fresh upturned soil of the grave with a black dress shoe. The maple-colored soil was a stark contrast to the well-groomed grass surrounding the grave of his fallen comrade. A ragged breath escaped his lips. Logston, Shots, and Phillips had stood shoulder-to-shoulder, flanking him. He was proud to call them his brothers-by-bond.

The Mayhem Managers were all navy chiefs, and they managed mayhem by their work ethic and know-how. They succeeded in balancing and leading their crews. They set the standard of excellence for an effectively running team against insurmountable odds of budget cuts, lack of man-power, unrealistic timelines for work orders, and the constant turnover of captains. They inspired others through their struggle to be the best, to have pride in their work, and the personal integrity that demanded they be better than the day before. The Mayhem Managers fought the fights that had to be fought in order to show others that there was always a way to improve.

Bliss couldn't believe Wagner was gone—his friend, his brother. He could still hear the deep echo of Wagner's crisp, clear laugh drifting through his bar. All the joking, all the conversations, all the cards games, all the workouts, all the partying together on deployments was at an end. Bliss recalled the first day he'd met Wagner five years ago. Bliss was on the well deck of his hovercraft when Wagner drove up in a Hummer and asked how it needed tied down. He wasn't afraid to ask for help or let an opportunity pass to learn something new. Bliss had loved that about Wagner.

The four men had silently paid their respects to Wagner. Clad in their dress blues, their chest medals glistened in the sun as it shone between the branches of a formidable-looking evergreen.

"I don't understand why we weren't notified of the funeral or service of any kind," Shots had said in a low, composed voice. He bent down next to the headstone and ran a hand over the engraved name.

"Maybe his family didn't want us here," Phillips said in a choked voice. "His mother, Master Chief Wagner, hated us. Always thought we were a distraction to him and his advancement."

Bliss's brows pulled at the center, and his chest tightened from the truth of it. He wouldn't say it out loud, but Wagner's death was laid squarely on his shoulders. He closed his eyes and the sound of the ambulance siren rattled through his mind. He could feel the cold air against his skin as he stood watching flames bellow into the night sky. He didn't know until the next day there had been two fatalities, one being his friend. He still couldn't believe the drunk driver had come from his bar, that he'd missed seeing the man leave. He blamed himself. But that wasn't the worst part: the drunk driver who'd killed one of his best friends played darts with Bliss only hours before.

He sent up a silent prayer for his friend. *From this life to the next. Brothers by bond. I will see you again one day.*

Out of nowhere, Bliss was hip-busted so hard he nearly got a face full of floor, and he was jolted from his memory. Thank God for quick reflexes. "Dang, Chrissie, slow down," he grumbled, righting himself.

Dark chocolate eyes met his and grew round with surprise. "Sorry, but you're in my way, Chief. Why don't you go have a beer with Dumb, Dumber, and Stupid over there?" Chrissie pointed to the other side of the room.

A roar of laughter near the stage captured his attention. He smiled and he shook his head. Dumb, Dumber, and Stupid. . . the perfect names for his friends. Phillips, the lady-killer of the group, scowled, not even slightly amused at Logston sitting across from him. Logston, his scarred face twisting, plucked away erratically on a guitar. Shots, a country version of Clark Kent with bright blue eyes, had his hand clamped down on Phillips's shoulder, holding him in place.

This can't end well.

"Earth to Chief," Chrissie snapped. "I'm trying to make money. Do you want me to cut my turnover rate to half because you're in the way?" She pitched her hip and shot a look at the guy waiting for his drink.

Chrissie was a no-nonsense woman, so Bliss decided to help her out. He stepped up to the ice sink, filled the scoop, and dropped the ice into the glass she held out to him giving her a wink.

"That's what I thought you'd say. You're all action and no talk. If only there were more of you out there, then maybe I'd think about keeping a man in my life." She sighed wistfully.

The guy waiting on his drink raised his hand. "I'm a doer, not a talker. How about you pick me?" he said, an easy smile playing at the corners of his mouth.

"Save it, money man. I'm working." Chrissie flashed her pearly whites then dashed off to grab the Jack Daniel's and a can of Coke. Not fifteen seconds later, her customer paid for his drink, then wandered off with a bruised ego to mingle.

Bliss settled back against the wall and surveyed the room.

"How's it going, big boy?" came Sarah's silky voice.

He played dead possum as his head bartender came into focus, her round, full breasts resting on the bar top in front of him. He was tired of the constant Sarah-a-thon.

"I'm here," he replied, refusing to stare as she leaned over the counter to steal a Bud Light. She squeezed her breasts together under the flimsy red top to draw his attention.

While he didn't stare, he did briefly admire her beauty for what it was—a weapon to be used against the weak of heart. He was not weak of heart, but she never learned. He wasn't on the market, in the market, or anywhere near the market. Not until he was retired in four years if he didn't stay in until the thirty-year mark. He had a fling here and there, but being in the military for sixteen years, he'd seen countless relationships crash and burn around him. Some couples didn't last a deployment.

"Why don't you come have a beer with me, big boy?" she said, popping the top of her stolen beer on the edge of his new countertop.

He gave her a dark look, curling his fingers into fists, and fighting the sudden urge to reach across the bar and grab the bottle from her hand. Instead, he popped his jaw and shoved his fisted hands into his pockets.

Pressing the bottle to her blood-red painted lips, she swallowed deep and moaned softly. "Mmm . . . please?" She batted her long dark lashes at him seductively, looking very much like the Playboy Bunny she longed to be.

He could've laughed at her attempt to manipulate him, but he wouldn't be cruel. No matter how pissed she made him.

"I'm bouncing tonight. Phillips is getting ready to sing," he responded.

Sarah rolled her sky-blue eyes dismissively.

"Have to peel the ladies off like a day-old Band-Aid," he said shrugging, concealing his irritation. Unfortunately, she was to be his stand-in manager once his sister Rose went on maternity leave. He couldn't afford to rock that boat.

Sarah uncurled from the bar and fussed at her denim miniskirt. She concentrated her obvious frustration on her clothes instead of him. She lifted her chin, threw her hip to the side, and said, "Your loss, baby. You know where to find me. I'll be with my girls." Then she flipped her golden blonde hair over her shoulder and twitched off, shoving through the crowd.

From the other end of the bar, he heard Chrissie's pixie laugh. He frowned, his eyes level under drawn brows. She'd been watching their exchange and was amused. Funny, he didn't feel the same, so he turned his back on her. She only laughed harder.

"All pains in my ass . . . just wait until the time is right," he grumbled.

Glancing at his watch, Bliss cupped his hands together, placed his lips on the slot between his thumbs, and blew a train whistle sound that carried over the crowd. His friends turned their attention to him. It was a signal they used to call each other from across the concrete apron at the unit.

He pointed to Phillips and tapped the face of his watch signaling it was time for him to get on stage and sing. Phillips bent across the table and yanked the guitar out of Logston's clutches. Phillips turned to walk away, but at the last second, he raised the guitar by the neck and bashed the butt into Logston's nose, and there was an unmistakable crunch of bone and blood.

Phillips hopped up on stage and clasped the microphone, smiling wickedly at his friends. "Think twice before you touch my guitar and poke fun at me."

Logston flipped Phillips the bird. Blood dripped off his upper lip. "Just wait," he threatened." He cursed under his breath, then ripped a napkin in half and shoved it up his nostrils.

Shots slapped the table as he burst into laughter.

Bliss just shook his head again. He was used to these antics.

CHAPTER THREE

The sunset blazed from behind the unremarkable-looking two-story house, bathing it in a soft glow. The California air was different from the Oregon mountain air. It smelled salty and as if she couldn't get enough air into her lungs. Her eyes raked over the other houses in the neighborhood. The yards were tidy and squared away. The houses were all the same color, as if wearing uniforms. Mathew had bought the house and had wanted her to decorate it, but she'd come up with some flimsy excuse to not travel to see him. That was three years ago.

River squared her shoulders as her brother had so often told her to do, stomped up to the front door, and slipped the key into the lock. Her hands shook.

Taking a deep breath, she opened the door and flipped on the light switch, but she couldn't move past the threshold. Her legs felt like lead. She tried to move, but the truth was that she didn't want to. *Come on. Mathew was your brother. Go in.*

Forcing her legs into gear, she stepped inside and closed the door. She dropped her backpack and sank to the floor, burying her face in her hands. She should have come months ago. The room had a faint smell that reminded her of Mathew. Slowly, she looked up.

The ceiling was vaulted in the living room. Pictures

sprinkled the walls. Mathew loved photography. He had a thing for covering every inch of wall space with pictures. She never understood why he hadn't pursued photography as a career path.

The pictures were of people she didn't know, places she'd never seen. Ten years he served as a marine. He'd joined when he was twenty-one. He'd been around the world six times. She'd always envied his appetite for adventure.

On the far side of the open living room, high up on the wall, was a black-and-white photograph. She grabbed a bar-stool from under a countertop and climbed on top, stretching to her full height of five feet nine inches, but the picture was just out of reach. In frustration, she snatched a flashlight from the countertop and tapped it against the bottom of the picture frame, knocking it off the wall and into her hands.

In the picture, Mathew was in his fatigues sitting on the hull of a ship, staring out at the ocean. The sun was casting a glow just before it sank into the sea. His eyes were pinched at the corners. His lips pressed together. He was sad, and he looked hauntingly alone. She touched the picture in a loving caress. Why was he sad? What was making him hurt? A tear fell onto the glass. Someone else had been there to capture this moment.

She ran her fingers over his face. "I'm sorry, Mathew. I wasn't there for you. I left you long before you left me." Tears streamed down her cheeks. It was a beautiful picture, one she would take home with her.

River curled into a ball on the black leather sectional and held the picture close to her heart. Her breathing was uneven, choked by her grief. What was she going to do without Mathew's two-hour phone calls? He always had the best stories about what happened at work or with his friends. He had been her window into the outside world. Working from home made it easy to isolate herself. Her friends from college visited now and then, but they were all getting married and having babies. It seemed everyone was on that path while she—at age twenty-eight—was single and stuck.

She curled tighter in on herself. The police report folded in her front pocket dug into her skin. According to the report of the vehicular accident, a witness had been standing at the crosswalk when she saw a large red F150 truck belonging to a Tyler Smith swerve and jumped the median. The truck drove into oncoming traffic and smash into a black Toyota Tacoma, Mathew's truck. Another witness report said a man had seen the red F150 from a block down the road swerved onto Main Street before the accident occurred. Tyler Smith's alcohol level was three times the legal limit. An officer had found several beer cans and a smashed bottle of whiskey in Tyler Smith's truck. No matter how hard she tried, she felt like she was drifting in this fog of disbelief, but here in this house, it was starting to feel real.

How was she supposed to get through this? Going through Mathew's stuff, deciding what to keep and what to donate? Her breath felt short and rapid, and black spots dotted her vision. She couldn't breathe. She needed to get out, to escape, to leave this place.

She got up too fast and stumbled into the leather chair. She blinked her eyes, willing the room to stop spinning. She grabbed her wallet and keys and left the house, somehow locking the door. The fresh air still felt weird, but she could breathe easier. It all felt too overwhelming, too much for one person to handle all at once. She'd seen a restaurant at the end of the block. Her stomach responded to that thought and she realized she hadn't eaten.

Her feet left Mathew's driveway and guided her down the suburban street, around the corner, and down another street and then another. She was lost. There was no restaurant at the end of the block, nor was there anything in sight. Her lip quivered as she almost burst into tears, but then she spotted a neon sign across the street: The Whiskey-Tango Foxtrot. Mathew's bar. She took a step closer. He'd talked about it many times. She didn't know it was so close. She wanted to see it. She wanted to go inside and be close to Mathew in this small way. So she did.

River pulled the hood of her sweatshirt over her face, shielding her roaming eyes from view. With a plain black sweatshirt, fitted jeans, brown leather steel-toe boots, and her hair tucked away, she looked like everyone else in the bar on a Thursday night after work.

She knew his friends hung out there, but she didn't know any of their names because Mathew had these crazy nicknames for them.

Pee Wee . . . that was his nickname for River. He called her that because she was smaller than him. It wasn't until seventh grade she finally caught up. But that summer he grew another five inches. Making it impossible to be anything other than his Pee Wee.

When she entered the bar, her heart screeched to a halt . . . then it went from zero to sixty. She pulled in a leery breath. People were clustered about, boisterous and loud. She didn't let the sinking feeling in the pit of her stomach deter her. She wasn't walking in the dark alone. Sure, people were drinking and even getting drunk, but she wasn't alone. Walking out to a car alone and at night would be a different story. It could set off her anxiety. But she was safe here, she told herself, and she was willing to ignore her nagging negative thoughts to see what Mathew liked about this place.

Spotting an opening, she stepped up to the bar. "Can I get a Coors Light, please?" she asked the bustling bartender.

"Sure thing, honey. That'll be two bucks. Happy Hour." The bartender moved with lightning precision, as if she'd been working in this bar her entire life. River was intrigued. In college she'd worked for the school press as an editor. It had been fun, but she didn't have any interesting stories other than how stressful it was if any work was late. The bartender probably had some great stories worth writing down. For the first time in days, River's curiosity was sparked.

River pulled out a five-dollar bill and tossed it on the counter as the bartender handed her the cold bottle. "Keep the change."

The bartender took the five-dollar bill. "Thanks, honey, have fun."

As River clasped her beer, she wondered if the bartender knew her brother. Were they friends? Should she ask? Her throat suddenly felt tight. No. She couldn't ask. She would start crying and she didn't want to make a fool out of herself.

The space was large with a stage toward the back, big enough for a five-man band. The bar lined the right side of the room, and four pool tables stood off to the left. The decor reminded her of a Friday's cracked out on military memorabilia, minus the food. River's stomach growled. *Food would be nice, even bar food.*

She placed herself strategically in the far corner by the bar where she watched the joint get packed, standing room only. A hum of chatter filled the room, drowning out the sound of pounding waves on the shoreline less than a hundred yards away. Minutes passed, and the alcohol saturated her blood. She was such a lightweight when it came to drinking. She relaxed a little, the Coors Light taking some of the edge off her grief.

A dreamy man with a guitar in his hand hopped up on stage and sat on a stool. River's eyes grew round. Back home, the only male she saw on a regular basis was Joe. He delivered her groceries twice a month, and he was as wrinkled as a raisin. Every now and then she'd spot a handsome face on her daily run, but she was all work and no play. She leaned back to enjoy the view.

"You ready for some kick-ass music tonight?" the dreamy man said.

"Yeah!" yelled the crowd.

River's lips pulled at the corners a bit, but a smile never formed. Her heart ached endlessly these days. She wondered if she would ever smile again . . . and really mean it. As her thoughts began to turn gray, her favorite song drifted over the crowd, "Sweet Home Alabama." A memory of her brother singing this song when they were younger colored her graying world with splashes of love.

Mathew was around fourteen at the time, singing like a crazy person with his right leg jetting out in front of him. He strummed his leg like a guitar, jumping from the sofa to the recliner. He'd been trying to make River smile after their mother scolded her over her grades. "What have I done to end up with a child such as you, River?" her mother would say. Mathew always tried to cheer her up, doing his best to make her laugh.

Just then, a rude voice ripped through the memory. "Get off the stage. You suck ass! Come on. Let's hear some real music," a woman yelled. She was a blonde Barbie type wearing a red top with a plunging neckline that displayed the cleavage of her large breasts. She wore a short denim skirt and three-inch red heels showcasing long, tanned legs. The woman's oval face was painted with heavy makeup. Her eyes were a sky blue.

River's eyes narrowed at the disrespectful woman. That one was trouble with a capital T. Two other women stood around a table with the blonde. Both were dressed in similar fashion. People stared at the blonde. No one smiled or laughed at her rude scoffing.

The blonde flipped her hair back and forth, laughing

heartlessly at every little thing, calling more attention to herself. The woman was ruining River's favorite song, and now River's irritation turned to full-blown disgust and anger.

Just then, a large man with a rough-looking scar on his cheek approached the blonde. River pegged the man as a country boy. He walked with confidence in his stride. She could spot these types fast if she knew what to look for—raised on a farm or a ranch, knowing the value of a hard day's work. River didn't have time for a man, but she could appreciate a good one when she saw him.

She leaned forward, wanting to eavesdrop on the conversation between the blonde and the scarred man, straining to hear what they were saying over the music. Acting against her better judgement, she left her seat and moved one table closer. She stood behind a group of men who were also watching the scene unfolding at the table next to them.

"Evening, ladies." The scarred man nodded.

"Yes?" replied the blonde without even bothering to look at him.

How disrespectful. River took another step closer.

"I want to buy you ladies a round of beer," he said, unruffled by the woman's rudeness.

"Sure, you can spend your money on me. I'm worth it. But you can do it from over there," said the blonde, pointing to the other side of the room.

Her friends shared uneasy glances but remained silent. What was their deal? Didn't they care their friend was acting like a bitch? And why was she so nasty to the guy?

"No disrespect, but I was talking to the ladies." He smiled at the brunette next to the blonde.

The blonde's nostrils flared, and River knew something was coming. The blonde teetered back on her three-inch heels as her hand swung back to strike the man in the face.

River didn't know what came over her, but she latched

onto the woman's arm, pulling her off balance just enough to slide in front of the scarred man. "Don't you even think about it," River spat, shoving the blonde back.

Her blood boiled. She didn't know these people, didn't care about them one way or another. But she was just so angry at the world. Angry that her brother was dead. Angry that her mother was cold and unloving. Angry that she allowed her anxiety to take over her life. Angry that she had been trapped in her home for three years, and of her own doing! And now she was free to roam, her actions erratic and feral. She felt like a woman possessed, unable to control her emotions, but it was liberating to have a target.

The blonde cried out and River braced herself. The blonde leaped for her like an alley cat, claws and all. She caught the blonde easily by the waist and shoved her to the floor. The woman landed in a growling heap. She tried to launch herself once again, but her high-heeled shoes made it impossible to move fast enough. River shoved her down onto her back, then quickly straddled the woman. Her knees clamped down on the blonde's shoulders, forcing her arms to her sides.

The room suddenly sounded muffled, as if she were underwater. River tuned out the noise, focusing on the blonde squirming under her. *Just breathe.* She clamped down on the woman's arms harder.

⁓⤳⧽

The music stopped and Phillips's mouth hung open. "Catfight!" he shouted, pointing toward the mob of people.

"Shit!" Bliss spun on his boot heel, anger welling up inside him. He had no tolerance for fighting in his bar. He shoved through the crowd. A moment later, he stumbled into an open circle. To his surprise, he saw a small hooded figure sitting on Sarah's chest, pinning her down.

He was impressed.

Sarah kicked and bucked, shrieking like a dying bird, but the person didn't budge. Anger morphed into concern for Sarah's safety, breaking through his stupor.

"I'd think twice before you try that again," threatened the person straddling Sarah.

"Get off me. You're going to be sorry," Sarah yelled, arching her back high.

"Sorry for what? Putting a rude bitch in check? Never."

He rushed over and roughly hauled the person off Sarah, surprised at how easy it was. Sarah was a panting, growling mess on the floor. Her hair was tousled, but there wasn't a scratch or bruise on her smooth, golden skin. He sighed with relief. If she'd been hurt, no one would hear the end of it . . . ever. He reached out and caught her hand, helping her to her feet. He gathered her into his arms for support. He almost felt sorry for her. *Almost.*

Bliss peered back at the person responsible for the assault on Sarah. The black hood had fallen away, revealing long, straight chestnut hair. The scent of lavender and apples rolled off her, causing his body to harden in all the wrong ways with Sarah still in his arms. He was certain she would get the wrong idea.

Logston anchored his meaty arm around the assailant's waist, dragging her lean body against his. "I want to watch that again. Never thought a woman would want to save me. What a turn-on." His dark eyes roved dangerously over the woman.

"Get the fuck off me!" the woman shouted, and she quickly squirmed out of Logston's grasp.

"Whoa, whoa, whoa," Logston said, holding up his hands in defense. "Didn't mean anything by it."

Bliss studied the woman's face. Seconds passed and the outside world receded. His mind blanked. Wide hazel eyes consumed him. Fear—stark and vivid—glittered in them. They darted nervously from him to Logston. Mixed feelings rose in his chest: concern, irritation, and a twinge of unwanted possessiveness.

She heart-shaped face was framed perfectly by her straight, shiny hair. The corners of her mouth turned upward, more than they turned down. That, as well as the high cheekbones, made her desirable. She remained motionless as she regarded him with fear, and there was something else in her eyes . . . was that sadness? Without warning, she twisted like a trapped feline and dashed for the exit.

He glared at Logston, uncertain of what to do. Part of him wanted to follow, but the responsible, honorable part of him that was a chief told him to keep his ass put. He had to contain and *control* the situation.

Letting out a frustrated growl, he focused on restraining his anger when Sarah demanded his attention.

"Maddox, call the cops," she whined, wiggling her soft body against his hard one. "I want to press charges."

He glared at her. "Get over it. She didn't hurt you and the woman was right, you're being rude. People are here to listen to Phillips, not your mouth!"

"Bliss," she cried, sliding her hands up and around his neck, resting her head on his shoulder.

His hands tightened around her wrists and peeled her off. "You're fine," he said.

She pouted, eyes sneaking a look out from under her lashes. A hint of a smile pulled at her mouth. *Shit,* he thought, *this innocent act of kindness will take a month of detached cold- ness to undo.*

"I think I'm in love," mumbled Logston. "She was trying to save me from getting slapped by Freddy Krueger over there."

Sarah hissed, fingering her disheveled hair. Logston

grinned, pleased with her reaction.

Bliss tapped down his impatience and signaled Phillips to begin playing. He fired up his guitar right where he'd left off. Then, he turned to Logston. "Take care of Sarah. See if she needs any ice."

"Like hell I will. She doesn't play nice. She's lucky I don't take her over my knee and give her the spanking she deserves."

"You asshole. Go ahead and try it. See how many testicles you have when you're done," Sarah warned.

Logston's nostrils flared, and he gave her a snort and then glowered at Bliss. They exchanged hard looks for a second, and Logston caved. "Come on, you can buy me a drink, and I'll rub some ice all over your sexy body," he said, taking Sarah's hand and dragging her off.

Bliss caught a smile breaking across her face and heard a soft chuckle rumble in her chest. He popped his jaw. The woman was beyond infuriating.

He marched toward the door. WTF was a combination of risks, liabilities, and constant mayhem, all of which he struggled to balance against his need to succeed in all things.

⚘

River burst from the building into the dark parking lot, her heart slamming against her ribs. She could see the Boise River, and she was suddenly transported to another place and time. She was walking to her dorm room. It was a Friday night. Most of the school plus half of the Boise area were at the football game, but she had a night class. Mathew had been gone for a year.

Darkness surrounded her as she walked the path next to the river. Her backpack, filled with books, weighed heavily on her shoulders. Distracted by the sound of the Boise River and her upcoming assignment, she'd missed the sound of someone coming up behind her. Suddenly, she was harshly yanked by

31

the waist and heaved off her feet to be body slammed into the dirt, just within the bushes. Her face pounced off the ground and everything was black for a few second. The black was chased away by the burning of her lungs for air. The weight of her book as well the person pressing on her was too much to breathe. She gasped for air.

"Hey there, pretty little thing," came a rough voice, words slurred together. "Want to have some fun?" Her cry of terror was drowned out by the roar of the stadium crowd not far away. The smell of beer was overwhelming when he tried to remove her backpack and grip her better. She clawed at his face and thrashed her body to get away. He tried to shove her back into the ground, and in their struggle, her fingers found a rock, and when he tried to flip her around, she bashed it into his temple. He stumbled backward. She scrambled to her feet and ran as fast as she could. She never told anyone, nor was she able to place his face. It all happened too fast. But she would never forget the sound of his voice and the smell of his breath.

She blinked back to the present moment, reminding herself that she was safe. That the man who was holding her tightly in the bar wasn't her attacker. She hated when the memory triggered. She heaved a sigh of relief. She'd managed to escape. *Focus. This is manageable.* A loud hysterical laugh leapt from her throat. It was official. She'd lost her mind. She wanted as much distance from the bar and the man with the scar as she could get. The man's size . . . his arms wrapping around her waist, the way he pressed her against his body. . . She shook her head dislodging the images and the sick physical sensations. The ghost of fear crept up her spine and she moved faster across the parking lot. The realization of what she'd just done caused her to tremble all the more.

She didn't know what had come over her. It had all happened so fast. In one moment she was on top of the blonde, and the next strong hands had grabbed her and forcefully pulled her away and restrained her. But she couldn't take her eyes off the man who'd broken up the fight. Black cropped hair and a tanned, raw-boned face. She swallowed hard as her body flooded with warmth and her nerve endings tingled. There was something slightly wicked about that face. Maybe it was the strange contrast of his eyes—a light golden amber—with his dark hair.

She couldn't believe the raw emotion she'd felt when their eyes met, and she'd felt this savage, consuming need to take him in completely. His black shirt strained to conceal a tempting, attractive male physique. River had become breathless and lightheaded.

And now she was racing across a parking lot heading back to Mathew's house. Half way across the parking lot, she heard footsteps trudging toward her. *Please don't be the guy with the scarred face . . . please, please . . .*

Glancing back, she felt on the threshold of a full-blown panic attack. The man came to a halt about a yard away. They looked sideways at each other. It was the scary good-looking man wearing a grim expression.

"What was that?" he asked in a grudging voice, gesturing back at the bar.

She didn't know what to say or if she wanted to say anything at all. She was fully aware that what had happened in the bar was unacceptable and embarrassing.

"That woman . . ." Her voice cracked. "I wanted to listen to the music without her mouth running off . . ." She was rambling. *Crap. In and out. Breathe.* "When *Scarface*—" She threw a hand over her mouth realizing what she'd just said. Her cheeks caught fire. "I'm sorry. That wasn't . . . I didn't . . . when the man with the scar came to the table, the woman tried to slap him, and I just couldn't stand there and do nothing."

Scary Good-Looking didn't seem to buy her excuse. His handsome face scowled. "You're going to have to do better than that," he said. Running a hand down his face in exasperation, he suddenly looked very tired.

Did he have to deal with this kind of thing all the time?

River lifted her chin. "It's not for you to understand." Of course she wouldn't tell him that she had no control over her emotions, that her body and fists seemed to have a mind of their own.

Scary Good-Looking raised a brow. He crossed his arms and thumbed his chin. "If I recall, you were sitting on that woman's chest, pinning her to the floor. If you ask me, that's not normal behavior," he said with a smirk.

She ground her teeth. "Why does she get to stay and I get followed out?" she asked, trying to stay calm.

His eyes narrowed. "Fighting isn't permitted at the Whiskey-Tango-Foxtrot. I won't have innocent bystanders getting hurt because of somebody's short fuse."

They stood there staring at each other. More than the words, River resented his tone. *Who was this guy?* Judging by his size and commanding air, he must be the bouncer. She glared at him and pressed her lips together. "I'm soorr—." She stopped. No, no apologizing.

Scary Good-Looking peered at her for an eternity, trying to make up his mind about her. Finally, he said, "I don't want to see you back in there for the rest of the night."

Her cheeks started to burn. He was already leaving. He had actually turned his back and walked away. The door swung open and two men pulled out some smokes. She could hear people laughing inside. Scary Good-Looking looked back at her. She thought he seemed sad, but why? He disappeared into the bar.

River's walk down Main Street toward her brother's house was a blur. The air felt stale when she entered the house, and once again a wave of sadness overwhelmed her. Her stomach rumbled, and she felt the urge to vomit.

She raced to the bathroom, groaned softly and placed a hand on the bathroom sink. She wrapped an arm around her waist, as her stomach rode a rollercoaster of unease she desperately wanted to get off. She gathered her wayward senses. *Am I having some sort of breakdown from Mathew's death?*

All those people, the scarred guy touching her . . . anxiety central. Why she thought going into WTF would be better than here, she didn't know. Dropping her head back embarrassment heated her entire body. Those people could have known Mathew, been his friends. She sighed, hollowness in her heart echoed needed to connect with Mathew. She would go back and apologies tomorrow. She couldn't live with herself if she didn't.

She bit her lip and stared at her reflection. The dark circles under her eyes reviled how sleep had eluded her for days. She walked out of the bathroom, and over to the closet and held a few of Mathew's shirts to her nose, breathing in his scent. Her eyes instantly burned, and she let the tears flow. Mathew was gone, but her heart just couldn't accept it yet. She took a final whiff and returned the shirts, arranging some of his things, which were out place.

Time heals everything, they said. She just didn't think it could.

River stepped out of the way as a large male with a shaved head and tattoos running up his jaw to his cheek glared exiting WTF. A small blonde with a large baby belly was hot on his tail. The strength she emitted didn't lessen her femininity. "Thanks for coming in. I will let you know about the job by the end of the week." The woman waved but as soon as he was out of sight she blew out a disgruntled breath, thin lips bouncing off each other making a childish noise.

River smoothed her skirt worried now wasn't the time to come and apologies for last night's behavior.

"Hi there, are you my next interview? I thought he was the last one but I have been forgetting everything with this pregnancy." The woman said in a cheerful voice River hadn't expected.

"No. I came to apologies for my behavior. Last night I . . ."

"Why what happen?"

River cleared her throat and lift her chin. "Last night I came to check the place out. A woman was being rude while a young man was singing. I . . . I . . . don't know. We got into a scuffle. The bouncer wasn't happy with me. I'm so embarrassed. I wanted to apologies to whoever was in charge."

"The bouncer. Oh . . . I see. That was you, humm." The woman circled, an interest etched in her expression River didn't understand.

"I'm impressed. There are few who would challenge Sarah. Her being a bitch and all."

"Right! Well I normally don't go around acting like that. Lately I have been under a little more stress than I am use to and I just wanted to hear the young man sing."

The woman stopped in front of River. "Do you need a job?"

"No. I have a job, though I have taken a leave of absence."

The woman wrinkled her nose. "Where are you from. Because it isn't from here. People don't come back and apologize for misbehaving at a bar."

"I'm from Oregon."

"What are you doing here?"

"I'm." A knot formed in River's throat and she pulled in a slow grounding breath. "Oh. I don't know taking a break from life I guess."

"Perfect."

"Excuse me?"

"You will be just what I need to keep Sarah in check. Follow me." The small but round woman walk into the bar and down a narrow hall.

River hesitated, not sure what to do next. Finally, she was in motion. She spotted the woman disappear into a room.

"Please have a seat."

"What for?" River asked, sitting stiffly in front of a desk.

"You're getting an interview."

The woman shoved a clipboard into River's hands with an application stuck to it.

"Stay here. I'll be right back." And then the woman was gone and River was alone. Her mouth hung open not fully grasping what just happen. Thoughts rammed full speed into one another and exploded. *What the hell did I just walk into?* She filled out the application in a rush trying not to think about what she was doing. There were times in her life when autopilot kicked in under stress and things got done and she didn't even know how. This was one of those moments.

CHAPTER FOUR

Bliss shot up the stairs to his apartment above the Whiskey-Tango-Foxtrot, taking three steps at a time. *Rose is going to kill me for being late for the interviews.* He shoved a hand into the leg pocket of his fatigues, pulled out the key, and opened the heavy front door. He was met by a bright, uncluttered loft. He cast a glance around the perimeter. All was as he'd left it. Clothes were laid out on the king-sized bed adjacent to the small gleaming white kitchen area. The beginning of a smile tipped the corners of his mouth, but it never fully formed. The gloom that had been cast over his life since losing Wagner choked him. Grief was an assassin striking, cutting you down when you didn't expect it. Today at lunch, Shots, Logston, and he had gone to the Subway on base. He'd walked in and couldn't breathe, remembering the last time they had all been there. Even though Wagner was a marine, they made time to have lunch together once a week. The three of them were already seated when Wagner arrived and walked straight into the glass door at full speed. They laughed as Wagner cursed his luck and tried to wipe his oil face mark from the glass.

Bliss didn't have much time. He flopped down on the edge of the bed and unlaced his boots. He kicked them off, then stripped off his uniform one layer at a time. His mind kept returning to last night and that woman with the long chestnut hair and hazel eyes. *Damn! How could a woman I'd seen once be so distracting?* He didn't like it. Earlier in the day, Shots had repeatedly asked him about the discrepancy list on hovercraft Seventy-Three as they did a walk through of the craft, and every time, his mind was elsewhere . . . dreaming about running his fingers through that shiny chestnut hair. It made him feel like a teenage boy. He had a crew to manage and a craft to keep running.

He dragged the shirt Rose had picked out for him over his head, scolding himself as he dressed. *This is why I don't have and don't want a girlfriend. I can't focus on work.*

As he slipped on his jeans, the sound of footsteps drifted in through the door leading up from the Drunk as Fuck or DAF room. It was the one major change he'd made after becoming a chief. He'd converted the garage connected to his loft into a holding tank of sorts when customers drank too much. His father had never cared if people left drunk only that they didn't start fights. He also punched a hole in the shared wall connecting the bar. Saved time not having to run around the building to get to the bar. He paused and looked over his shoulder. He could hear Rose's grumbling long before her round pregnant belly came into view.

He hurriedly thrust his feet back into his boots and laced them up. His hair was flat from wearing his cover, so he tousled it a bit. Rubbing his thumb over his chin, he could tell it was time for a shave.

"Made it by the skin of your teeth, I see," complained Rose, sounding out of breath from her climb up the stairs.

His half-sister wore a bright blue dress with a white sweater, her long platinum-blonde hair draped over her shoulder in a side ponytail. Her honey-amber eyes were focused on him. There was a distance in them he didn't like. Though they had different mothers, he and Rose shared the light amber eyes of their father.

"How's the kid?" he asked. He rubbed his hand over the tight muscles of his sister's belly. In the last month alone, she had doubled in size. He wondered if it hurt to grow so round, but he never asked. He didn't want to upset his sister. With women, weight or size was never a good topic to discuss.

"I'm sorry I'm late. I couldn't leave as soon as I wanted," he said as she avoided his gaze. After their fight last month about Chapman, her ex-boyfriend, things between Rose and Bliss had been strained. Rose had changed since being in a relationship with Chapman. She wasn't as confident in her choices when dealing with the bar and she was jumpy in a way Bliss didn't like. She didn't confide in him anymore like she used to. Mostly, she kept to herself and didn't come to see him unless it was about the bar. He didn't know how to fix their relationship, and it was killing him little by little every day. He missed her smile and how they poked fun at each other. He would do anything for her not to be mad at him.

"It's not a big deal. After all, you're the boss," Rose said weakly, looking very pale. His arm encircled her shoulders, and he felt a strong urge to protect her.

"How are you doing?" He gave her a soft shake. "The truth, Rose, no bullshit. Don't tell me what you think I want to hear." He kept his tone soft.

"Oh, I'm just tired, that's all," she said hesitantly. "The baby never stops moving—like all the time. I can't get any sleep. I just want him to come out. I'm tired of sharing my body. I just want it back, all to myself."

He would've chuckled if Rose hadn't sounded so pained. But he got the distinct feeling she wasn't saying what she really wanted to say. He let it go.

"I'm sorry the little man is kicking your butt. You know I'll help anyway I can."

Rose peered up at him, wrapped an arm around his waist, and squeezed. "Thank you. How about you take me for a ride on the Harley and we shake him out?" She batted her lashes. "I'll love you forever."

He squeezed her right back. "I thought you already did . . . and no way am I taking you for a ride. With my luck, you'd go into labor, and I'm not going to be delivering my nephew on the side of the road."

"You suck," Rose replied. Just then, a little kick hit him in the side. He glanced down at Rose's belly. He wasn't sure if he'd just been kick or slugged by the baby. Rose shrugged apologetically.

His chest ached. For a brief second, it felt like old times—before Chapman.

"It's your turn to interview. I haven't had any luck with my list. You get the last one. She is in the office already." Rose turned and wandered out.

Bliss sighed. He wanted to make things easier for Rose, but she won't let him, and it hurt. He knew if it weren't for their father's stupid bar, Chapman wouldn't have been able to worm his way into his sister's life. What made it worse was Chapman worked at the unit with him. He had to see him every day and not punch his face in.

⁂

Thoughts of the devilishly handsome man who had followed River out of the bar surfaced and bloomed. Again, warmth filled her body. She recognized it for what it was—trouble and ill-timed. Perhaps if she got the job here, she could work on healing some of the wounds she carried—old and new. She could meet some of Mathew's friends and connect with him in this small way. Whether she could talk about her brother without breaking down remains to be seen. Maybe this could be a good thing. She wasn't ready to pack Mathew's life up into boxes and leave it in a dark corner of her garage. It was too final. She needed time.

She tried to relax as her eyes drifting, searching every square inch of the office for hits about the owner of this place. Who would grill her with interview questions? The small woman had left to retrieved someone else, but who. It had been years since she'd had an interview, and this was for a job she had zero experience doing. This needed to be her best sales pitch ever if she was really doing this.

She released the death grip on her skirt and rubbed a hand over her tight chest. Her pulse rushed like an athlete in the last ten seconds of a big game. *You're fine. Everything is fine. Calm the hell down. Scary Good-Looking is nowhere to be seen.* A twinge of disappointment caught her off guard. She frowned. *What the hell is wrong with me? Do I want to see him . . . or not? All he did was scold me as if I were a child. Get it together.*

She tried to focus on the looming bookshelf that swallowed the entire back wall of the room. *Breathe. This is manageable. Oh yeah . . . manageable. I'm going to be a sweat pit soon.* She fanned herself.

Her eyes widened with delight when she saw the collection of books. Leaning forward, she ran a fingertip over the book spines. A shiver of excitement shot up her arm and did a jig throughout her body.

She glanced over her shoulder. *What am I doing? If I get caught, it won't be good.* But curiosity won as she snatched a random book off the lower shelf. She flipped the book open to a picture of a group of military men on a beach with a large vehicle behind them. She ran her fingers over the edges of the other pages. She looked closer at the men in the group, and her heart softened as she gazed at their faces. They were all smiling, arms thrown wide over each other's shoulders. *Brothers.*

Then she gasped, recognizing Scary Good-Looking and Scarface. River quickly closed the album, shoving it back on the shelf. Sitting on the edge of her seat, she rubbed her hands nervously over and over again in her lap. *Keep it together.*

The door flung open and River spun around, her heart jumping in her throat. Scary Good-Looking stood in the doorway staring boldly at her. She flushed. *Just cut me open and pour salt on my wounds.* She set her chin in a stubborn line and schooled her features into a hard shell of indifference. He was only a man—yes, a handsome, well-built man—but a man all the same.

He stepped into the room, a massive, self-confident presence. The door closed behind him with a click. His jaw was clenched, and his eyes were narrowed. She suppressed a shudder as he brushed her shoulder. A scent of oil, grease, and metal trailed behind him.

He sank into the chair behind the desk. She held her ground, met his stare, and gave him the biggest fake smile she could muster. Willing herself to breathe, she extended her hand across the desk. "River Connelly," she announced, trying not to sound as nervous and guilty as she felt.

He looked at her hand, making no move to shake it. "Maddox Bliss. You can call me Bliss or Chief. I'll answer to both," he said in a hard, stern voice that held no trace of friendliness.

Her hand dropped in embarrassment. They stared at each other in silence for several moments. *What does he see when he looks at me? A fish out of water, a frightened little mouse, a bug that needed to be squished?*

River felt dumb sitting there smiling like a loon. If he wasn't going to get the show on the road, then she would. She handed her application to him. His eyes swept over the paper. She fidgeted with the hem of her skirt and shifted in her seat. *This was a bad idea.*

"You want a job here?" he asked, as he leaned back in his

chair.

"Aaaa." She didn't know what to say to that, not really.

He raised a brow. River could see the annoyance in his eyes. It was also in the tight pull of his forehead and the discouraging tone in his voice. This was going to be a challenge. Oh, how she loved a challenge, anxiety be damned. Seeing him there like that sped her pulse and caused her to tingle with pleasure. She liked his grumpy face.

She bit her cheek and turned her head, pretending to look at the small green lamp near the corner of the desk. She knew she was playing with fire. River couldn't stand the awkward silence anymore. "Why are you looking for a bartender? Is someone leaving, or have you gotten busier and need more people?" she asked, finding her voice.

His nostrils flared. "You have no experience as a bartender." He sat forward, pointing at her application. "It says you 'work' for a publishing company as an editor, so I'm curious as to why you're here if you already have a job."

She ignored his question the same as he had done. Again, in her super-sweet voice, she said, "Do you need a bartender or not?"

His slick brows pinched and he frowned. She saw the calculation on his face. He wasn't a man to give information before he weighed it.

She pressed her lips and caved. "I took a leave of absence." She tried to look unconcerned by his obvious rejection. People applied for jobs with little to no experience all the time. "I want a break from editing. As you can see, I've been an editor quite a few years. I learn fast, and I'm not afraid of hard work."

"My sister, Rose, is the manager and she's going on maternity leave soon, and my head bartender is stepping into the slot, but it still leaves me with a hole. The position is temporary." His face softened a bit.

River felt a spark of hope. This could work. "Oh, that would actually work out great for me. I mean, a few weeks' break is all I need."

He pushed back in his chair, lacing his fingers together. "Is editing books not a lucrative career?" he asked sarcastically.

What a big, fat jerk. Her backbone turned to steel. A flash of anger melted her remaining anxiety. "Lucrative enough to buy my own home and support myself for six years. But I need a change, like I said. So you can ask me to leave, or you can move on to the next question."

He nodded. "Okay then, there's no need to continue this interview. I'm not even sure why Rose scheduled you to come in. Please see yourself out." Then he tossed her application into the trash.

River blinked hard, seeing red, and she shot up from her seat as if propelled by an explosive. "What the hell? Is this about last night? You big baby. I came here today to say I'm sorry. Then, then I was bamboozled . . . I think?" she yelled, leaning over the desk, getting uncharacteristically close to him.

He stood and placed his fists on the desk. "My problem," he growled, "is you."

Ha! I knew it. "I didn't know this was your bar. I thought you were the bouncer."

"That woman you sat on is the head bartender. It was her night off."

River clenched her jaw. "Does that excuse her for having horrible manners and no consideration for others?" She wiggled her finger in his face.

He laughed dryly. "If you're trying to scold me, don't bother."

Why did she have to have such a temper about that woman's behavior? *Stupid triggers. Always going off at the wrong times.* She could hear Mathew laughing. Yep . . . he would be laughing his ass off at her if he were here. She leaned forward, her fists now resting on the desk, her hair falling over her shoulder. Her eyes cut across his face, his teeth gritted together, but he didn't move.

"It's not good business having your bartender sitting around getting drunk where regulars can see her. And she sure as hell should be held to the same standards as all the other customers."

She did the unthinkable. She tapped him on the cheek and said, "Have a nice day." She grabbed her purse and stalked toward the door, body shaking, heat pouring off her back. The thing was, she didn't know if her anger was directed at herself or that insanely sexy, irritating man behind her.

As she was approaching the exit, the door swung open, nearly knocking River over. She sprang back just in time. The small pregnant woman burst in.

"Maddox, hire her now," the woman cried.

"Stay out of this," he said, irritation in his voice.

River was dumbstruck. What the hell was happening?

"Rose, you wanted me to interview . . . I'm interviewing."

"No, you're not. You're being an ass. I can hear you all the way out there." Rose pointed toward the bar.

"We can talk about this later. Ms. Connelly was just on her way out."

"Like hell she is. You're chasing her off." The woman's hand flew in the air in exasperation.

"Rose."

"Maddox."

The two of them were facing off, and River was right smack in the middle of what seemed to be sibling drama.

"Maddox, I'm going to have a baby in the next month. We have to hire someone. Chrissie and Sarah can't do everything themselves."

His head dropped. He stared at his desk. "Maybe I could

get off work early until you're ready to come back to work or you could reconsider a different candidate." He ran a hand through his hair, desperate to find another solution.

"Maddox, it's not that simple." Rose tucked a strand of white-blonde hair behind her ear. River glimpsed blue-green bruises around her wrists before her white sweater slid down to cover them. Did he see them as well? It was his sister, he had to see them. River searched his face for a sign. Nothing. How could he not see them?

Rose fought back tears and swallowed hard. "Look at her." She gestured to River.

River bit her lip. *Why are they talking like I can't hear them?* This was the most uncomfortable she'd felt a long time.

"She's well dressed and nicely put together unlike the others I've seen all morning." Rose waited, amber eyes probing. "I know what happened last night. I know she put Sarah in her place and that is important for anyone we bring in. And she has already done it."

Bliss slammed his fist against the desk.

"Maddox, please." Rose's voice broke into a thousand pieces, scraping River's ears with such sorrow she wanted to cover them. It was clear to her this woman was suffering.

Rose chased away her tears and straightened. Her face hardened. "Maddox Bliss, you hire her because . . . because . . ." Her voice broke once more. "I'm moving to Oregon to live with my mom, and I'm not coming back."

River watched for several seconds while Bliss soaked in what Rose had said. She saw pain in his eyes. She could feel her anger toward Bliss diminishing.

"Rose, she isn't looking for something permanent."

"People can change their minds, can't they?" Rose whispered.

"Fine. You want her, you got her." He locked eyes with

River. "Be here tomorrow at fourteen-hundred to start train-ing. Rose will be here when you show up."

River didn't know what to say. How could she say no to this woman who was in such an obvious dilemma?

Bliss walked out of the office, stopping briefly in front of her. They were almost touching. She held her breath as his intense eyes bore into hers, and her whole being seemed to fill with wanting. Her knees weakened.

Finally, thankfully, he left the room. She exhaled sharply, her tension easing up once he was gone.

Rose sat in the chair and burst into tears. River didn't know what to do, but the image of those bruises on the woman's wrist burned in her memory. The sobs that broke free from the woman was more than River could bear. She tentatively approached and rested her hand on Rose's shoulder. It was all she could do to comfort her.

CHAPTER FIVE

River glanced around the Whiskey-Tango-Foxtrot. Down the hall, she could hear someone vigorously typing on a keyboard, the frantic beat matching the rhythm of her pulse. She followed the sound to the small office where she'd been interviewed yesterday. The small, lovely, pregnant blonde who had forced Bliss to hire her was seated at the desk.

River relaxed as best she could. Rose wore a green sweatshirt stretched tight over a round belly. She sighed with relief at her casual getup. Wanting to make a good impression, she took her time choosing clothes for her first day. She finally went with a black fitted V-neck shirt, faded jeans, and Converse sneakers.

River opened the door all the way and stood silently fiddling with her shirt. She wasn't sure how to interrupt. Rose glanced up from her typing and threw a hand over her mouth, stifling a cry.

River swallowed hard and found her voice. "I'm sorry to startle you," she rushed to say. "I didn't want to interrupt. You looked busy. I'm River Connelly. We met yesterday. Mr. Bliss said to be here at two o'clock today to start my training."

Rose collected herself. She straightened her shoulders and cleared her throat. "Yes, I'm Rose Bliss, if you didn't figure it out yesterday. I'm the one going out on maternity leave, or I should say permanent leave." She swiveled around in her chair and gave a profile of her large belly. "As you can see,

I don't have much time left before I pop. I'm due August eleventh."

River could sense that there was more behind the light banter, but it was none of her business. "I can come back a little later if you're still busy."

"Don't be silly. I was working on the procedures for the bar. Let me print them out so you can have a copy. Use it as reference and you'll know your way around in no time."

Rose moved the mouse of her computer, and after a click here and there, the printer fired up. Rose turned and grabbed the papers when the printer spit them out.

"Sit, I need you to fill out some paperwork. Then I'll show you around." Rifling through a desk drawer, she took out a handful of additional papers. "Okay, let's see . . . a code of conduct needs to be read and signed, an I-9 needs two forms of identification—you can look at it and bring them tomorrow—a W4, and your own copy of WTF's handbook. Here's a pen. I'll be back in ten."

River took the pen and went to work. Fifteen minutes later the paperwork was filled out and she had scanned the handbook. Rose then took her on a grand tour of the Whiskey-Tango-Fox-trot.

"Okay, let's start at the back of the building and work our way out toward the bar area," Rose said, her voice weary. They walked down a hallway that funneled into a large room.

"This is the DAF room."

River's eyes swept over the space. It was an open room with light-colored walls and a high ceiling. No windows. Folded cots lined the walls, and rolled-up sleeping bags and pillows were tucked between the beds. A towel and bucket hung at the side of each cot.

"DAF stands for 'Drunk as Fuck."

Her eyes widened.

Rose smiled. "What? I didn't name it that. Maddox did.

It used to be a garage, but when he made Chief, he turned it into the DAF room. Oh, and by the way, you better get used to hearing profanities because the majority of men who come in here are military. Camp Pendleton is only a few blocks away and the LCAC unit."

River nodded, making a mental note. But wasn't sure what LCAC stood for.

"We have a four-drink max within two hours unless the person is buying for friends. So pay attention to who and how much you're serving because as I'm sure you can guess, this is where we drag the drunks. Not all of them, just the ones without designated drivers. Chrissie and Sarah are very good at asking who the designated driver is before they serve drinks. But every now and then, a loner shows up to meet friends and ends up in here. And then, on special occasions, a whole herd will come in and get drunk, knowing Bliss will put them up for the night." Rose rolled her eyes.

It seemed odd to own a bar and then have a room like this. It sparked her curiosity about Scary Good-Looking a.k.a. Chief Bliss. It was a good idea. Maybe a room like this could have saved Mathew if all the bars had them.

"Do they get mad when you stop serving them drinks and bring them back here?"

Rose shrugged. "No, most of them know we're trying to keep them from getting a DUI. So they let us drag them here so they can sober up. If they look like a puker, which from my experience most are, we give them a bucket to get sick in and a towel to clean up with after. I mean, most are grateful. What bar will go out their way to do that?"

"If you don't mind me saying, it's a bit of a contradiction." River swept her hands around the room. "A place like this, don't you think? They become your responsibility when you take them in. Isn't it also a liability to have them here alone after you close the bar? They could wander out of here and start drinking again . . . or worse."

"It's not much of a liability. Bliss lives above the bar." Rose pointed to stairs off to the side. "He checks on them. It must seem unusual, a chief owning a bar, making money off his fellow comrades, and then trying to protect them. He is unusual, to say the least. But he didn't buy this place. He inherited it when our father died six years ago." Rose's eyes turned glassy, and her words were choked off a little. "This wasn't our dream. It was our dad's. Maddox struggled with owning it for a long time, but it's hard to let a legacy go . . . when you lose someone you love. This is all that's left of our dad."

A cold numbness welled up inside River. She understood completely. Yet, that flicker of curiosity snagged on "our father." Rose and Bliss shared a father, but she wasn't sure they shared a mother based on what Rose had said yesterday. She was sure there was more to the story, but she didn't want to pry.

"It's made things complicated for us over the past few years." Rose shrugged. "But life is complicated. Come on, I'll show you the loft. There's not much to it, but Maddox likes it."

"No, it's okay. I believe you. I don't need to see his home. It would be inappropriate."

Rose smiled at River's protest, her light amber eyes sparkling. "Right . . . well, let's keep moving. I have a lot to cover before Sarah shows up and gives you the stink eye." She strolled out of the room and made it about ten feet before she noticed River wasn't following.

"Did he tell you everything I did?" River asked, her heart scuttling to a stop. *Would Rose react as unfavorably as Bliss?* Rose gave her nothing to gauge her reaction. *Dang, she's as bad as him.*

"No, Maddox doesn't talk about stuff like that. He's good at keeping his mouth shut. Logston, however, blabbed like he'd seen a prize fighter go down right in front of him. Called me right after. Had to blab to someone. Even wake me up. Men!"

"Logston?"

"Big, scary bald guy—tattooed, ugly scar on the right side of his jaw."

"Oh, yes," she replied. *The asshole who touched me and made lewd remarks.*

Rose stuck a finger out. "If you're smart, you wouldn't tell that man anything. He gossips worse than a teenage girl."

"It was terrible of me to have attacked the woman like that, regardless of how she was acting. Something inside me cut loose."

Rose marched back to her. "Don't sweat it. She was asking for it, giving Phillips such a hard time. She's always asking for it. Don't know why Maddox keeps her around, or why I put up with her as a friend."

River managed a weak smile.

"To be honest, I can't wait to see her face when she sees you."

Her eyes widened.

Rose waved a hand in the air as if shooing flies away. "Don't worry. She won't do anything to you. My brother will be watching her."

River felt sick. What had she gotten herself into? Seriously, she was behaving totally out of character these last few days.

"Come on." Rose nudged River. "Next is the storage room. You'll become very familiar with it since it holds all the alcohol. And you'll love this. It's alphabetical, so it's easy to find what you need fast, compliments of the boss's OCD. He's a compulsive organizer. I think he's a control freak. Anyhow, he's the label king, but don't tell him I said that. The vein on the side of his forehead will pop out, and you never want to see that."

Rose ushered her down the hall. River followed, pondering her situation. *Not another control freak, a micro-manager.* She'd dealt with her mother's control issues growing up, always clean and orderly, no room for imperfection. She wondered if it was a military thing. Mathew never exhibited any of his mother's controlling tendencies, but she hadn't spent much time with him after he left for the military. She really didn't know who he was before he died. Sadness felt so heavy in that moment.

The storage room was the largest room of them all, next to the bar area. And Rose was right. Every shelf, row, and box was labeled. It seemed like overkill, but she would learn ten times faster with all the help. Seemed like a lot of alcohol for an average-size bar. She could only imagine how busy it got. She swallowed. Busy meant a lot of people and messing up a lot of orders.

"Okay, let's make this fast. Chrissie will be here soon to start training you behind the bar." Rose walked over to the nearest shelf, which was a foot taller than her. "We order supplies every other week, and we make the distributors wheel the orders back here so we girls don't kill ourselves. Then you take the cases and place them on the shelf in the back, always moving the old stock forward. If you have less than three cases on a shelf, you write it down here. Got it?" Rose shuffled over to a clipboard on the wall next to the door.

"Yes, seems easy enough."

Rose laughed. "Just remember the procedure. It's on those papers I gave you. Maddox expects excellence 24/7, no exceptions. Protocol is protocol. Blah, blah, blah. Bloody military men. Always working my last nerve."

Before River knew it, two hours had passed, and Chrissie, the bartender who had served her the night before, a lean brunette with chocolate-colored eyes, was frowning at her, as she failed to list where everything was behind the bar . . . for the fourth time.

"I can't believe I'm having such a brain fart with this," River grumbled.

Chrissie laughed-snorted, then smiled, exposing her white straight teeth. "It's okay. We can do it again." She kept looking at her watch and messing with everything on top of the counter.

River was getting anxious as she went over the list in her head: *Drink glasses, top left shelf at the end of the bar, wineglasses overhead, ice machine behind me, limes, lemons, olives, cherries, salt at the garnish station, right top counter next to the sinks.* Then it hit her. Sarah was coming. It wasn't as though she could leave. Well, she could, but that wasn't an option.

Rose came out of the office. She glanced at the clock behind the bar, looking more irritated than anything else. "How's she doing, Chrissie?" she asked.

"Fine, may take a few days, but she'll get it."

River tried not to scowl at Chrissie. After all, it was the truth. Bartending was way harder than she'd thought. And she hadn't even started making drinks yet. She just wished it didn't have to sound so bad.

"Well, it's time to batten down the hatches, people," Rose said. "We have an MMI headed our way."

"What's that?" she asked, looking at Chrissie and then to Rose.

"Moody Man Incoming," replied Rose.

"That would be Bliss," said Chrissie. "He hasn't been in a good mood since the accident."

She caught Rose shooting Chrissie a "will you shut up?" look.

Accident? Did Bliss get hurt?

Chrissie gave her the peace sign with her fingers. "I'm taking a fifteen-minute break. I'll be on the patio chain-smoking until Bliss goes up to the loft and leaves us alone."

"Scaredy-cat," Rose taunted as Chrissie sailed by, packing her American Spirits on the meaty part of her palm.

"Right back at you, Preggo," Chrissie said with a chuckle. Then she opened the large glass double doors to the patio and a rush of hot air swirled into the bar. It felt nice against River's face. The sun streamed in and brightened the large room.

She didn't know how she felt about seeing Bliss. Maybe they could start over. Get some sort of re-do. *Something is wrong with me. A handsome man yells at me and I go weak in the knees at the thought of seeing him?*

"Ouch," Rose said, glaring at her stomach. "You listen here, kid. There's no room in there, so you either come out or stop pushing on my bladder."

River couldn't contain herself. A smile spilled across her face and a chuckle slipped out. It was a strange feeling, complete amusement mixed with a deep sorrow she couldn't shake. She brushed the feelings aside and focused on Rose. It was the funniest thing watching a beautiful young woman reprimanding her unborn child.

She placed a hand over her mouth to conceal the smile. She wondered how old Rose was, maybe twenty-seven or twenty-eight. What was Rose's story? How did she come to be at this point in her life? River rolled the questions through her mind like a ten-ton boulder. For the first time in a long while, she wanted to *really* know someone. A wave of guilt washed over her. She'd missed out all these years on getting to know people. She liked Rose and Chrissie; they reminded her of herself. She wasn't afraid of strangers after the attack, but her distrust in humanity had grown. The need to be out in the world had grown smaller. She liked working from home in her safe little bubble. But being here at WTF felt nice in a strange coming-home kind of way.

CHAPTER SIX

Bliss grumbled at his crew all day for not doing things the right way on the craft, or more accurately, not doing it his way. And his way was always the right way. His mood was so polluted with disgust that even he didn't want to be around himself. But he was tired of other chiefs not giving a shit about integrity or being accountable for their shit show of a hovercraft. He had two crews and two crafts to manage, two of which ran and were the most reliable crafts at the unit. Some chiefs sat in the office and bitched but never got off their asses and helped their crew get shit done. He loved working on the craft with his crew, but he hated being in the office. It was the change after making chief he could have lived without. He was a craft engineer prior to a chief; he'd been responsible for all the mechanical maintenance of the craft and putting in work orders to get parts. Now there was a lot of paperwork on top of managing, and some of his crew was reluctant to read a procedure manual. It drove him nuts.

He fumed, keeping a death grip on the handlebars of his charcoal-gray 1957 Knucklehead Harley-Davidson. Hot air smacked his face as he ripped down Main Street, tail pipes thundering.

Eight INSURV inspections in a single year. Outrageous.

A living nightmare. The only craft running at the Unit were in his detachment, and half of them were his responsibility. However, that wasn't the problem, not really. It was the craft that were getting ready to go through INSURV—they were pieces of shit from another detachment.

No one's craft ran like the Mayhem Managers' because they actually believed their craft were an extension of themselves—a reflection of what they could do. And now, the yahoos sitting on their asses who couldn't give two shits about their craft expected him and his guys to fix it all. His jaw clenched so tight he thought his teeth would crack. It was hard to deal with people who didn't operate at his level.

His frown deepened when he remembered that his day wasn't going to improve, no matter where he tried to push his thoughts. In five minutes, he would be at WTF confronting Sarah because of River. He couldn't believe he gave in to hiring River. It made his gut roll to think about how the control was snatched from his hands. He grumbled to himself. Anytime Rose started to tear up, it was over. He was a sucker when it came to his sister.

Then again, maybe River would work out. There was something about her—besides being the most desirable woman he'd ever laid eyes on—that made him think she could do the job. The way she tipped her chin at him showed she wasn't afraid of a challenge, and at WTF, challenges waited around every corner. Not to mention, Rose did have a point: she'd put Sarah in check. A smile spread across his face for the first time that day. He would never forget the sight of her sitting on Sarah.

He stopped at a light and for some strange reason, the memory of River standing in his office proud and stubborn penetrated his thoughts. Things never quite worked out the way he intended when it came to women. The last relationship he attempted to have was three years ago when he was thirty and settling down pulled at him. Savannah worked at the bar for about a year. She was a small thing, sweet, quiet. He'd taken her on a few dates and things had been going well for a few months, but then he had to deploy. He'd gotten up the courage to see if she would wait for him and she'd said no. Said she didn't want to deal with that. He'd been confused and hurt. He closed himself off after that, not willing to put in the effort only to be disappointed in the end.

The light turned green, and he drove two miles before pulling into the parking lot of WTF. Sarah's car wasn't there, which meant he still had time before she showed up and opened a can of pissed-off on him.

Driving around to the other side of the building, he parked in the alley and climbed off his Harley. He peered longingly at the outside steps to his loft. There wasn't enough time to change. To keep Sarah civil, he would have to be there when she arrived.

Worn out from a day's work in the sun, he stomped into WTF, unsure of what he would find. The cells in his body vibrated with a surge of energy as his eyes locked on River. He made it to the middle of the dance floor before Rose's voice stopped him.

"You're beet red," she exclaimed, shaking her finger in his face.

He blinked. Where did she come from? "Leave me be, woman. I'm not a baby," he said.

He couldn't take his eyes off River. His body hardened. She stood behind the bar, pressing against the countertop behind her. The snug, faded jeans and the black shirt that hugged her in all the right places made his mouth water.

"I wish you would use sunscreen and stop getting sunburned all the time. You're going to get skin cancer, and then the doctors are going to cut your ass off and paste it to your face. Then you'll really be a butt face." Rose laughed like a hundred cheering fairies, amused by her own joke.

He tore his eyes away from River. As he opened his mouth to respond to his sister, Sarah walked in, followed by Phillips. The room went silent. Everyone was eyeing one another.

Chrissie strolled in from the patio and came to a screeching halt. Her eyes locked on his, swept to Rose, then Phillips and River, but landed hard on Sarah. An *"Oh shit!"* was stamped on her face. With a grin, Chrissie pulled out a cigarette, mumbled something under her breath, and disappeared.

Nice, real discreet, like that wasn't going to send a warning flag to Sarah. He glared at Rose, beseeching her with his eyes to say something.

"Hi, guys. How's it going?" Rose said, acting as if nothing was going on.

"Good," replied Phillips, looking curious. He dragged everyone's attention away from River as he turned and approached Rose. "How's my big mama?" He placed a hand on her belly.

Rose seemed on the verge of protesting, but looked too tired for a fight. "I'm not that big," she said, swiftly knocking his hand away.

"What the hell is she doing behind my bar?" cried Sarah, pointing a slender hand at River.

Here we go. Bliss wished this day would be over soon.

Rose waddled over in front of Sarah. He turned and flanked her, blocking River from view. Sarah's eyes blazed.

"We needed someone to train, so here you go. Be nice and have fun," Rose said, smiling wide.

Sarah's eyes shot fire. "I'm not training anyone." She crossed her arms over her breasts like a teenager having a tantrum.

"Listen, this baby is coming soon. You'll train who I tell you to train," Rose ordered, her voice taking on a harder edge.

Sarah was unfazed. "She leaves, or I do," she said, lifting

her chin stubbornly.

Bliss knew this was going to happen. He'd told Rose she'd resign. He assembled every grain of kindness he could find to offer this irritating creature. He placed his hand on Sarah's shoulders and massaged them gently with his thumbs. Goose bumps rose on her soft skin. He could manipulate Sarah if he wanted to; he just never had a need to until today . . . and he knew he would regret it.

He took a deep breath. "Listen, we can't run WTF without you. But you know we need an extra hand when you're off shift. Chrissie can't work all your hours."

"Why does it have to be her? You saw what she did to me the other day."

He gazed at River. "We don't have time to be picky." His tone was harder than he'd intended.

An emotion he couldn't place shadowed River's features, but only for a second before her chin lifted. An odd feeling nudged his brain. In that moment, she reminded him of Wagner with that dark hair and stubborn chin. He shook it off and looked back at Sarah. Her sky-blue eyes were dark. Her lips pouted. He knew she wanted the one thing he would never give her. He could never be more than just a friend. In truth, he didn't even want to be that. She wrinkled her pointy nose and looked over his shoulder.

"Fine, but if she can't carry her weight, then she's out. I don't care if Rose spits out triplets."

He squeezed her shoulder. "Thank you."

Sarah batted her lashes and then wrapped her arms around his neck and kissed his cheek. "You're welcome, baby—anything for you."

CHAPTER SEVEN

"Bliss, for the love of God, can we please play darts?" Phillips raked his fingers through blond spikes, frustrated. "If you're going to stand there and stare at the new girl . . ." He paused, face scrunching. "What did you say her name was?"

"River," Bliss said through gritted teeth.

"Right, River. Not that she's hard on the eyes or anything. I mean, I'd take her home. But damn, you got crazy stalker plastered on your face." Phillips flicked his wrist effortlessly and a dart sailed through the air, striking the dartboard. The group of guys playing next to them clapped and cheered him on. "See, they're interested in the game, and they're not even playing with us. Which is more than I can say about you."

Bliss ignored him and rolled a red dart between his thumb and index finger, eyes locked on the women moving behind the bar. "I'm not staring at her, you jackass. I'm making sure Sarah doesn't pull a *Crouching Tiger, Hidden Dragon* and launch herself into the air and attack." He slung the dart from between his fingers, hitting the board dead center. Phillips's black dart flopped to the floor. The group next to them erupted in laughter. That would shut Phillips up for sure.

He smirked to himself as he watched Phillips deflate as he stared at his dart on the ground. He didn't have to watch River to know where she was. Since she'd stormed the beach that was his life three days ago, his senses had been thrown into overdrive. He'd never been more aware of a woman's presence in his life. He shifted uncomfortably at that realization. Attraction was one thing, a relationship another. *Not happening.*

"Damn it, I don't know why I even said anything. The only way I can win is when you're distracted. Go back to staring and give me a chance," Phillips complained.

He shrugged. "You wanted to play."

"Yeah, yeah, my mistake. I thought it would be fun." Phillips flopped into a nearby chair, extending his long legs out in front of him as he leaned back. "Not a bad crowd for a Saturday," he said, peering around the room.

Bliss followed his gaze, still holding two darts in his hand. People buzzed around, stopping to chat here and there. It was a good night for River to train—just enough people to keep her busy, but not enough to skyrocket her stress level for a first day. He tossed the remaining darts on the table next to Phillips, then spun a chair around and straddled it, resting his arms over the back. He glanced at River once more, his shaft hardening.

❧

If Bliss didn't stop staring at her, she might actually get pissed enough to throat chop him. River pulled in a rough breath. She could feel herself sinking in quicksand. She wiped her sweaty palms on her jeans and lifted her chin with determination. *I can do this. I refuse to fail.* Before she dashed out from behind the bar to clean some of the tables, Chrissie clasped her arm.

"You don't look so hot. Stop stressing."

"I'm not," she lied.

Chrissie raised a brow. "Sell that to someone else. I have eyes. Don't let Bliss get under your skin. He's just a control freak, and lately he hasn't been able to control things the way he likes to." She let go of her arm and frowned. "Do you want me to bus the tables?"

As much as River wanted to say yes, she didn't. Her therapist would be proud of her, putting herself back out in the world. She lifted her chin higher and hurried out from behind the bar with a tray and a rag tossed over her shoulder. She rushed to an empty table near the back. His eyes stayed on her; she could actually feel them on her skin. Placing the tray at her hip, she carefully placed the beer bottles on to it. *Please don't mess up. Don't drop anything.* Next, she grabbed the rag off her shoulder and wiped the tabletop. One of the bottles started to move. She went rigid, took a breath, and placed a finger on the mouth of the beer bottle. She glanced at Bliss. His expression was blank.

She went to the next empty table and cleared it. Hurrying back to the bar, she returned the used items to their rightful places. She hurried to cleared the three remaining tables.

⁓

"When are you going to pay me to sing again? I think I'm getting a following, even started my own fan page." Phillips looked all too pleased with himself.

Bliss eyed him. "You hard up for money?"

"Me?" A look of disgust crossed Phillips's face. "I like singing for the ladies, you know that." Bliss rolled his eyes. "How about next Friday? That's if we're not all at the hospital with Rose."

Bliss scrubbed a hand down his face, not wanting to think about his sister. He needed to talk to Shots, tell him about Rose leaving, but Shots wasn't here. Phillips was the next best person to talk to. He would talk to Shots tomorrow.

"What's on your mind?" Phillips sat up, placing his forearms on his thighs, green eyes tight with concern.

He exhaled, trying his best to hide the sorrow and frustration weighing down on him. "It's Rose."

"Worried about her having the baby?"

"Yes and no. Not the way you're thinking."

Phillips tilted his head to the side. "Does it have to do with your suspicions about Chapman being rough with Rose?" he asked.

"You got it. Rose had bruised wrists a few days ago, and she's all jumpy again." He lowered his head and began to rub his temples. "She said she's leaving."

"So, what're you going to do?"

"What can I do that won't have me going to Captain Mass and getting busted down a rank?" he said.

"Mmm . . . don't know what to tell you, brother, other than give it time. Leaving may be the smart thing for her to do with the baby and all, especially if Chapman is still coming around the bar. I would miss her for sure, but I would understand. I'd visit her . . . hell, we'd all visit. Where's she going?" he asked, yawning.

"Oregon. I think that's where her mother is. I never kept track of Tracy after she left Rose here with me and my dad. There was no need to. My dad lost all respect for her walking out on her four-year-old daughter. I can still remember my father's expression when Tracy slammed the door in Rose's little face. I don't think he ever really thought a woman would do that. My mom died, but Tracy just walked out . . ."

"I hate to say it, but sometimes things turn out better when a parent leaves. It is better than listening to fights and them disrespecting each other like my parents did. Besides," Phillips leaned forward, "if it hadn't gone down like that, you would have grown up without a sister."

Phillips had a point. Bliss's life would look different without Rose in it.

"Oregon. Hmm, winter. Snowboarding, here I come."

Phillips glanced at his watch. "Well, I've got laundry to do. Not to mention, we have a shit ton of work to do on Monday. If you're smart, you'd let the ladies close up and hit the sack. You're going to need it."

Phillips pushed to his feet and gave him a slap on the back. "See you at Oh-My-God in the morning on Monday. That is, if you won't be going to our usual Sunday run. The Physical Readiness Test is coming around. We really shouldn't opt out for a few weeks."

"Sure. See you in the morning," Bliss said.

"I'll text the guys when I get home." Phillips strutted over to the bar and tapped on the counter. He winked at the ladies and pointed to the door. Chrissie waved good night, and Sarah rolled her eyes.

Bliss heaved a sigh. Phillips was right. Monday was going to be a long day at the unit. If he deprived himself of sleep tonight or tomorrow because of River, no one would want to be around him.

Unable to resist, he watched her for a little while longer. His eyes roved over the curves of her body. She was a feast for his eyes to feed on. Her high ponytail drew his attention. The ends brushed her flushed cheekbones as she grabbed glasses for Chrissie and Sarah. There was hesitation in her every move. She flicked her hands constantly, curling her fingers in and out, and then wiping them on her pants. The first few times he'd watched her do that, he thought it was nerves. But obviously it was a habit.

He peered at Sarah, who seemed to be ignoring River, making it apparent that her training would come from Chrissie. Not a problem. It would give Chrissie a chance to share what she knew. If she did well at training River, he would give her a raise.

Deciding it was safe to leave Sarah, he made his way up to the loft to get some sleep and to think about how he could talk to Rose about the bruises. If Chapman was still around, it would take everything in his power to not hunt him down and kill him.

River clutched the door handle and shook it with all her bottled-up frustration. Locked. *What a bitch.* Sarah told her to take a few bottles to the back and this was what she did, locks her in.

As she struggled to control herself, her hands fell to her sides like wet noodles, all her remaining energy spent. Hot tears burned her eyes. It took so much from her to work in a place crawling with people, but she'd sucked it up as best she could and made it through the night. Talk about a crash course in therapy. Being locked inside the bar by Sarah, however, was more than she could handle.

Pressing a hand to her lips, she stifled a whimper. What was she going to do? Did she have to wake up Bliss? Hell, no. She didn't have the energy to deal with that stubborn man on top of it all. He'd watched her like a hawk half the evening, waiting for her to mess up no doubt. She was grateful that he was nowhere to be seen.

Her thoughts drifted to Mathew and the last time they'd talked. He wanted her to come to California and stay with him.

"Come on, River. If you don't come to see me, I'm going to start thinking you don't love me anymore," Mathew whined as if he was ten.

River slapped the book she'd been reading on her leg as she lounged on the couch for the night. "Oh, get it together, Wagner. You're starting to sound like our mother."

"You did it, you went there. I can never forgive you. I'm going to hang up the phone. I'm crushed."

A smile broke across her face with a bark of laughter. "So

dramatic. I told you I have been busy with work."

"I know . . . I just miss you." His voice softened.

Part of her cracked a little knowing he was sad. "Tell me about work. Anything exciting happen?" she asked, fighting down her own pain.

"Not really, just went to WTF and had a drink, played some pool with the guys."

How she wished she'd come sooner. She shook her head. "I'm here now," she said out loud, her words echoing around her, bouncing off the empty caverns of her heart.

She gazed around the space. Her brother was dead, and she was alone. But she would find a way to move forward, even if it meant working with Sarah. Maybe being in this situation would save her thousands of dollars in therapy.

Figuring she would rather die than wake up Bliss, she kicked off her Converse and pulled out her ponytail, shaking her hand through her hair. She tucked a strand behind her ear. Her stomach growled. Food. River tippy-toed down the hall to the storage room. She'd seen some chips when Rose showed her around. She snuck into the storage room and snatched two snack-size bags of chips and a bottle of water from a shelf. Then she left three one-dollar bills on the counter.

Happy with her loot, she headed for the comfiest-looking booth that lined the back wall. She stretched her tired legs out over the seat and wiggled her toes. Her feet ached. Tonight had been the longest she'd been on her feet since college. Most of the time, it was her bottom that ached from sitting too long at her desk. She took a long drink, letting the water refresh her tired soul. A little of heaven in a bottle. *What a day* . . .. She tore open her first bag of chips and lifted it to her nose; chips had never smelled so good before.

"What a great dinner," she said to herself, munching away. She started to relax and even found herself enjoying being alone in the dark. A sliver of moonlight cast its trail along the floor. The pounding waves outside were music to her ears. She liked it. It calmed her. She hadn't thought about all the things she could do being near the ocean. A flicker of excitement touched her veins, and she caught herself wanting to smile. She could learn to surf, go for a walk, or run on the beach. She hadn't run since she received word of Mathew's death, which wasn't surprising. Mathew had taught her the power a run could have. He'd been her running partner since high school. He would push for a hard run when she was upset with friends or her mother to burn off the emotions, and when she was happy, she would jog slow and let the good mood soak in. It was her release. Tomorrow she would go for a run.

Her thoughts drifted over all the faces she'd seen tonight and wondered how many knew Mathew. Scrunching her nose, she recalled a few of the nicknames Mathew had used. There was Twinkle Toes, the Chief, Pretty Boy, Ms. Sassy Pants . . . she reached for the a few more, but they headed for higher ground. She closed her eyes trying to form mental pictures for each name. She chuckled as a male face, smooth and feminine, took hold for Pretty Boy, who had shaggy blond hair like Fabio.

"May I ask what the hell you think you're doing over there?" His voice boomed from the hall.

She jumped and sucked in a breath full of chips, choking on the crumbs. Her heart tripped over itself as Bliss's honey-colored eyes stared at her from across the room. He was shirtless, and his black boxer briefs hung low on his hips. *Awkward.* She took in his maleness. *Beautiful.* She felt her body soften, and she didn't like it. *No, no . . . I'm not going to like him. Lust after him maybe, but that's it.*

She cleared her throat, and her chin came up. She was ready for a fight. "Sarah locked me in. Can you believe it?"

"Yes. She isn't nice."

"Then why let her work for you?"

He looked thoughtful for a second. "Sarah is complicated."

Crazy is a better word. River looked away.

He strolled over to her booth and sat down, not caring in the least that he was half-naked. She shifted in her seat; a wave of unease started to rise when she realized she was locked in with a half-naked man she hardly knew in the middle of the night. She couldn't help but look at him. Muscles rippled everywhere, and he looked utterly delicious. *Oh man, why does he have to look so good?*

"I wasn't sure what to do, so I got something to eat." She held up the bag of chips. "I paid for them. Look . . . over there." She pointed to the counter where her money was visible.

He stole the second bag of chips off the table and tore into them.

"Hey, those are mine. I paid for them. I didn't say you could have them."

He smiled, and it took up his whole face. "Go get another one from the back."

She didn't move from her spot and just stared at him. What was it about this stubborn man that appealed to her?

He laughed. It was a rich, full sound that reminded her of Mathew. She found herself wanting to smile again, and the corners of her mouth tipped a little.

"Tell me what you thought of your first day on the job," he said, crunching on his stolen chips.

This was a side of him she hadn't seen before. It felt odd because she didn't feel like the cornered rabbit she normally did with strangers.

"Okay, I guess," she said, taking a sip of her water.

He watched her so intensely she forgot to swallow and the water ran down her face. He smiled as she mopped her chin with the edge of her shirt.

"Fair enough. Did Sarah or Rose give you a schedule yet?"

She dug in her pocket and retrieved the paper Rose had given her, along with her notes. "Yeah. Looks like I'm off tomorrow, and then I work all next week from five p.m. to two a.m. I think it may take me a while to get used to staying up late."

He raised his brow. "Why's that?"

"I'm a morning person. Never been much of a night owl." She picked at the label on her water bottle. "Rose is very nice. You said she was your sister in the interview."

He finished his last chip and then flattened the bag on the table. Pride danced in his eyes, but then there was a flicker of pain. She remembered Rose was going to leave.

"Yes, we have the same father."

"Do you have any siblings?" he asked.

Yep, there it was. She chewed the question over and over again in her mind. The thing was, she really didn't know how to answer that anymore. Her brows stitched together, her head tilting to the side. She regarded him for a short while, wondering how to respond.

"No," she finally said. Her voice cracked.

His eyes narrowed. Could he see? Could he sense the lie? If he could, he didn't press the subject, and she was grateful.

"Word to the wise, when you're closing with Sarah, make sure you get out of here before her. She locks everyone in. When she's done, she's done. Understand? You're the only one without a key. Sarah has locked Chrissie in a few times too before I gave her a key, so don't take it personally. After the third time I finally had to give a key to Chrissie."

"Noted." *And yeah right, it's totally personal.*

He scooted out of the booth and quickly disappeared down the hall. He reappeared a minute later, striding over to the front door. He unlocked it, shoved it wide open, and gestured to her.

She shimmied out of the booth and grabbed her shoes, not bothering to put them on. She hurried to the door with long, purposeful strides, glad to be excused from the conversation. The closer she came to him, the tighter her muscles locked together. Her heart thumped. After brushing past his hard body, she stopped in front of him, looking out into the dark parking lot, having doubts about leaving. She didn't know if she could walk out there by herself with no one as a witness if something happened. She swallowed. At least Mathews was only a few blocks away. A rental car sounded really good about now.

"Good night," he said in a husky voice that warmed her blood in an unwanted way. He pushed the door wider for her to pass. Before she took another step, he dipped his head and smelled her neck. It was slow and deliberate. She could feel the sexual magnetism that made him so self-confident. There was a tingling in the pit of her stomach, and then he shoved her out the door, locking it behind her.

She stood there holding her shoes. What just happened? Had he just shown interest in her? Did she care? Had he merely bent to open the door wider? Her thoughts collided and left her confused. She peered around the dark parking lot, trying not to think about the creepy homeless people or drunks who could be hiding in the shadows.

Hurriedly, she tugged on her shoes and ran across the parking lot. She glanced back at WTF, and there he was standing at the door, watching. Oh, thank God at least he could witness her murder. She tried to shrug off what just happened, but every feeling under the sun followed her home.

CHAPTER EIGHT

Bliss pulled in a deep breath and held it while he waited for Rose to answer the door. When she did, he assessed her appearance. Her eyes had dark rings around them and her hollow cheeks made her look like a ghost. Not seeing any new bruise, he let out the breath.

"What're you doing here, Maddox, it's Sunday?" Rose pulled at the sleeves of her sweatshirt and he scowled. There was no reason to beat around the bush with his sister. That wasn't the kind of relationship they had. Always to the point, even if it cut deep.

"Those are why I'm here." He pointed to her wrists. "Don't think I haven't noticed them."

"What're you talking about?" Her eyes darted this way and that, never able to look him in the eye.

He reached out and took her hand, then pulled up the sleeve. The bruises were less purple and more green now. "The bruises."

Rose yanked her hand back. Then she grabbed Bliss by the shirt and jerked him into her ground-level apartment. "Want some coffee?" she asked.

"No. I want to know what's going on." He pulled out one of the chairs to her table in her baby-blue-painted kitchen and sat down. Making it clear he wasn't going anywhere soon.

Rose sat down across from him. Head hung low. "What do you want me to say?"

"Are those from Chapman?" He clenched his teeth. She didn't answer. "You know how I feel about him. I told you months ago when you started dating him that he was trouble." A fist hit the table causing Rose to jump. *Shit.*

"There's nothing to worry about, I promise. I have it under control." Her tone was hard, determined. "I don't need your help. I can take care of myself."

"Clearly, that's why you're leaving for Oregon."

Pain flashed across her features causing her to look much older than her years. Bliss cursed under his breath. He knew Rose was tough; he had helped make her that way. He just couldn't get his fear in check.

She pushed to her feet, her bellying bumping off the table. "If you're here to give me a lecture about my life choices, save it. It isn't anything I haven't already told myself." She pointed to the door. "It's my day off, so go away."

Bliss stood. "If he's physical with you, I can report him to the command. It doesn't have to go to the police."

She turned her back to him. "Have a good day."

He walked out, slamming the door behind him. He fired up his motorcycle and drove back to WTF. He didn't know what to do. He wanted to respect Rose's "stay out of it" declaration, but she was pregnant. What kind of man—what kind of brother—would he be if he didn't do something?

When he made it back to WTF, every muscle was tight. He didn't know how he was going to get through his run with the guys. Shots was in the parking lot.

"How did the interviewing go for a new bartender?" Shots asked. He was tugging on his New Balance shoes from the tailgate of his black-lifted F-150 truck.

"As good as it could go!" Bliss suddenly didn't want to talk about it. He swung his arms from side to side, working the tension out of his back. He gazed out at the waves. The sun coated his bare skin like warm butter. He soaked it up for a moment. Surprised that Shots hadn't pressed for an explanation, he eyed him suspiciously. Always digging, always trying to understand people, that was Shots.

Against his better judgment, and to save time, he said, "Rose got mad at me." He waited.

Shots's sharp features became animated. He howled with laughter, black hair falling onto his forehead. He hopped off the tailgate and slapped Bliss on the back.

"What did you do this time?" Shots asked, peeling off his shirt and exposing his farmer's tan.

Instinctively, Bliss raised his arm, blocking Shots from view. "Good Lord, man. Put your shirt back on. You're going to blind everyone who comes within a ten-yard radius."

"Helps to clear our path," he said playfully.

"How? They'll go blind, fall to their knees, and then we run them over?"

Shots snorted. "Nice try on the subject change. It's a no-go."

Just then, Phillips arrived. Only Logston was needed to get the show on the road.

"Remember the girl who pinned Sarah to the ground on Thursday night?"

"Oh baby, do I—all those curves and those eyes." Shots fisted a hand and then pretended to bite it.

Bliss found himself uncharacteristically annoyed with his friend.

Shots threw his hands up. "You can't tell me you didn't think she was smoking hot when her hair fell out of her hood. I mean, hot damn. I almost fell off the chair I was standing on."

He'd been so captivated by River that night he hadn't noticed anything else.

"She works at the bar now, started Saturday."

Shots's jaw dropped. "How the hell did that happen? I mean, I love a pretty face, but what about Sarah?"

"Apparently, she was the best applicant Rose had seen in the interviews."

Shots's blue eyes brightened and he smiled. "Did Sarah's fangs come out when she heard? Fire leapt off her head, right? Can't believe I missed all the fun because I was standing duty."

Bliss jabbed Shots in the shoulder, hoping to give him a dead arm, but Shots bobbed and weaved out of the way, looking very much like the fighter he was—swift and graceful. Bliss knew firsthand. He'd seen Shots take down this big marine two deployments back when they had hit port in Singapore. One hit, Shots danced around the guy and then bam on the floor the guy went. Wagner called him Twinkle Toes after that.

"Someone's in a bad mood," Shots criticized. "We better run soon, or you'll be no fun at all today. Wait, let me rephrase that: you're never any fun."

Shots had no idea. His life was shit in a pink handbag. He thought about Rose. He didn't have the heart to ruin his friend's day by telling him about her leaving or the bruises. He had long ago suspected that Shots had a thing for his little sister. He stiffened, unsure of how he felt about that. Regardless of Shots's feelings, he decided he would wait until tomorrow.

Phillips approached sporting blue shorts and a bright yellow shirt that read "Navy" in a reflective print.

"What, you too lazy to get real running gear? You have to wear PT gear instead?" Shots mocked.

"Why not? It's made for workouts," replied Phillips, looking unconcerned.

The corners of Bliss's mouth twitched up. He wanted to leave his troubles behind him for a little while and enjoy his friends. It had been weeks since they'd ran together outside of PT, and he wasn't going to waste his energy worrying.

Shots leaned over and took a whiff of Phillips. "You stink! Did you wear that for physical training this Friday?"

Phillips nodded.

"You're not Tinker Bell like Wagner said, you're Stinker Bell. Stay in the back. I'm not absorbing your funk for the next six miles," Shots said hastily.

Bliss's mouth dried at the mention of Wagner's name.

Phillips stretched in front of Shots, invading his personal bubble, lunging forward on his right leg, hands over his head. "Fine with me. I'm sure you'll smell like roses when we're done."

Shots sent Bliss a you-have-to-be-shitting-me look. "Why are we friends with this smartass?" he asked.

"Because he's entertaining, and I don't have the energy to irritate you like Phillips does," he replied seriously.

Phillips glowed in satisfaction. "Yeah, I'm your own personal irritant—lucky you!"

Bliss shook his head and tuned out the sounds of Shots and Phillips as they began their daily ritual of aggravating each other. He looked toward the beach. A four-foot wave crashed on the shore, and he noted the lack of bodies. He was pleased—fewer people to dodge. His thoughts turned to Rose as he toed the sand on the boardwalk. What was it going to be like without her around?

Logston, with his long-legged stride, popped out from behind the lifeguard building. "Ready to do this?" he said. Finally, they could get their "run on," and the two bickerers would be forced to shut up.

"Sure am," Bliss said, clasping his friend's hand. Logston pulled him in close to give him a shoulder bump.

"Let's go," Logston commanded, silencing the squabble of the two guys.

And just like that, they were off as a group, trotting over

the soft pale sand.

Bliss set the pace in front, and Shots fell in beside him. His stride wasn't as long as Bliss's, but Shots's tree-trunk legs had little trouble keeping up. Phillips and Logston fell in behind.

It took about a mile before each hit his stride perfectly within the group. As they ran along the water's edge, Bliss stared off into the distance, fixing his gaze on the Holiday Inn where they would turn and double back. Running was the only time his thoughts drifted in and out like the tide. When he ran, his mind was a place where nothing could take root, but today he was consumed by thoughts of Wagner. This was the first time the guys had run together without Wagner. Wagner would run backwards and say, "Come on, guys, you run like a bunch of Billy goats." Bliss had never understood what the heck he meant by that. Goats could be fast when they wanted to be. He frowned. Maybe that was the point. He would never get the chance to ask him.

Breathing became a challenge as his emotions welled up. Nothing was going to be the same without Wagner. He had let his friends down because he had failed to keep them safe. The man who'd killed Wagner should have never left his bar after consuming so much alcohol. Heck, the man should have been cut off long before the end of the night. His eyes burned. He let the thought of Wagner go and it was replaced with Rose. He cursed the day his father had left him the bar. He didn't want it, but Rose had said she could run it and she had. She'd done a good job for a long time. Then Chapman happened. He pushed his body to set the pace a little faster, not wanting to think about Rose or Wagner.

As the miles ticked by, he spotted a curvy brunette running a short distance in front of them. A high ponytail skimmed her defined shoulders, which set his heart beating to an erratic rhythm. They moved closer to the woman. As the sound of their pounding feet rose into the air, the woman turned and her hazel eyes flicked back at them. It was River. He groaned inwardly. He couldn't believe his luck. She was like a beefsteak he wasn't allowed to have the night before his PRT, but she just kept showing up to torment him.

She sped up and pulled off to the side, as if wanting them to pass. He knew it was best to simply cruise past and continue on with their run. He did just that. He sped past her, and from behind he heard, "Good morning, beautiful." Logston sounded pleased.

He fisted his hands and glanced over his shoulder. Logston had slowed and was now running next to her. She nodded and bit her bottom lip.

He felt a grinding irritation scrape over his bones. He popped his jaw and slowed the group, not willing to leave Logston behind. Shots glanced at him confused, yet followed suit. He broke away from Shots and paced himself behind River. He caught Shots peering at him, an amused look touching his features. He sent Shots a keep-your-face-shut glare. Shots straightened and continued to run as if nothing was happening around him.

River stole glances at the group as they clustered around her. She acknowledged Logston and Phillips and gave them a smile. It made him want to curse. Her eyes met his. *Finally, some attention.* Her chin lifted, and she frowned. Her reaction made him grin.

"Good morning. Nice day for a run," she said to Logston.

Logston hooted at her. "It sure is, and the scenery is great."

"I wanted to apologize for running off so abruptly the other night. I was embarrassed after my behavior with Sarah."

"Don't sweat it, beautiful. And thank you for standing up for me."

River flushed slightly, and Bliss felt his pride get pricked. His gaze roved over her intensely, aware of the strength she emitted. Every lean muscle could be seen working in her upper and lower back. Her tight, round bottom flexing with every stride. A light breeze blew his way and her scent of lavender and apples found him. Every cell hummed. Her scent was becoming his personal drug. Suddenly, he noticed her shoulders and back tense slightly, and she pulled forward about a foot in front of the group. Shots and Logston matched her stride.

It happened several times before it hit him: she was either trying to get away, or she was challenging them. There was hunger in her eyes. For him? No, not for him. She pulled forward again. It was definitely a challenge. Excitement coursed through him and he accepted it.

He pushed forward, matching her stride for stride. After about a mile, they were running in full sprint. He heard Logston and Phillips panting hard behind him. He didn't think they would last at this pace much longer, and he was right. Not six strides later, Logston was bent over and gasping for breath, and Phillips was lying on the sand on his back.

He clenched his jaw. Being a natural-born sprinter, he kicked it up a gear and pulled up beside River. Shots leaned forward, watching them closely. Bliss didn't know why, but a smile broke across his face. River didn't see, or perhaps she did. She was staring off into the distance, determination lining her face. What was she trying to prove?

He nodded to Shots, and the two of them pulled forward, away from her. Shots was smiling now. This was the most clean fun they'd had in a while.

Just when he'd thought they had her beat, she burst through a hole and smoked them both. A smile lit up her face. It was the first time he'd seen her really smile. It was breathtaking. He might have been a natural sprinter, but distance was his downfall. He had repeatedly trained to run six miles, but his body was telling him he was at his halfway point. He needed to slow down now.

Shots started to fall back, sweat running off him. He too bent over and waved him on. River had picked off another one of his friends. She continued to run effortlessly.

River's eyes sparkled mischievously and a laugh exploded from her lips. It was the richest sound he'd ever heard. Right then, he knew. He couldn't outrun her. She must have a jet engine hidden inside somewhere because she was the fastest thing he'd ever seen.

He was stubborn, but he lost, no matter how you looked at it. He slowed down to a walk. Seeing that he had yielded, she too slowed down.

"Sorry, I got carried away. It's been a while since I've pushed myself like that. I hope your friends will recover."

His jaw dropped. He didn't believe she'd said she'd been out of practice. *How fast was her usual running pace?* Only the word *wow* came to mind.

"They'll live. It was good to have someone push us for a change."

She shifted from foot to foot, shaking her legs, not wanting to stop moving. She began to stretch. He couldn't tear his eyes away from her. Shots eventually limped up to them, holding his left ass cheek.

"What was that?" Shots asked her. "You're the fastest chick I've seen."

She gave Shots a sexy smirk, then stretched out her legs as she cooled down.

Moments later, Logston and Phillips materialized.

"I like her," said Logston. "Can I keep her?" He wagged his brows up and down at her.

She flushed again, looking uncomfortable. Logston was the last person Bliss wanted to compete with for a woman's affections. Not that Logston was doing that now, but he knew his friend's appeal.

"It feels good to run. I used to run all the time and really pushed myself. But then I got busy with work and only jog a few miles in the mornings. I wish I hadn't stopped after college."

"Hadn't what? Gotten busy with work or jogging?" Phillips asked, brushing his blond hair back.

Bliss didn't interrupt the easy conversation taking place around him. He wanted her to talk. He wanted to know more about her.

"Both I guess." She raised a hand out to block the sun. "I'm that way." She pointed toward the pier. "I have things to do. Thanks for the run."

"No. Thank you," Logston said. Then he told her his number. "I go by Logston, but you can call me baby, stud muffin, whatever you want."

"Or Beef Cake," Phillips said.

She pressed her lips together as a look of curiosity crossed her expression. "Have a good day," she said, walking away from them. "Beef Cake . . ."

Bliss was filled with disappointment. *Would it have killed her to stay a little longer?*

Acting on impulse, he hurried up alongside of her. "Can I walk with you?" he asked, trying not to sound as pathetic as he felt. Interacting with women had never been his strongest suit. He knew he was a good-looking guy, but that didn't mean it came with the gift of charm, so he didn't try. He left the smooth talking to Logston and Phillips.

She eyed him wearily. That wasn't the reaction he had been looking for. "It's a free country," she said, pushing a few loose hairs out of her face.

Damn it, if that wasn't the sexiest thing he'd ever seen. She didn't like him. Every red-blooded male liked a good challenge now and then. He had to observe and find her weakness.

The sun danced in and out from behind the morning clouds that rolled in.

"I think we need to start over." He stopped and touched her arm gently. Her soft skin lit fire into his veins. She looked at his hand and shook it off. He took a step back.

"Hello, I'm Maddox Bliss." He held out his hand to her.

A thoughtful look crossed her face, as if she was analyzing this new turn of events. After that moment of hesitation, she took his hand and said, "River Connelly, pleasure to meet you." She rolled her eyes as her hand slipped from his. He had amused her. It was a good start.

They both moved toward the boardwalk.

"So, River Connelly, how did you learn to run like that?"

～✦～

River wasn't sure what Bliss was trying to do, but the topic seemed safe enough. He'd surprised her by asking to walk with her, especially after shoving her out of the bar last night. Maybe he was feeling guilty and wanted to make nice. She chewed the inside of her cheek. She had to admit this side of Bliss was terribly and dangerously attractive.

"I ran cross country in high school. Worked on distance before I started pushing for a faster time in college."

"Why do you like to run?" He walked onto the boardwalk and stood there looking at her. He seemed genuinely interested. She didn't know what to think. With his shirt off and his shorts low, she found her thoughts wandering.

Run, what? Oh, yes. She stepped on the sidewalk, and his firm hands grabbed her waist, yanking her against his granite chest. Her heart leaped.

"Watch out, asshole," Bliss snarled at a man cruising by on a bike.

"Check yourself, I'm riding here," the skinny man shouted as he rode past them.

Bliss had one arm wrapped around her. She didn't move. She couldn't. She was rooted to the spot from fear . . . and it was a lovely spot to be rooted in. Heat radiated off him, and his rough fingers grazed her lower back. Dipping just under her shirt, they seared her skin. Her body stiffened, out of her control. She gazed at his hard chest, his neck, his ear, and then his face. He was looking at her, and there was fire in his eyes, smoldering, ready to burn her if it could. She shuddered in his arms. He didn't back away. She cleared her throat, and the sound seemed to cut through his thoughts.

"Sorry. I didn't want your first run on the beach to end badly."

"Thanks."

He stepped back, and his hands dropped to his sides. The moment was gone. She shook off her fear, praying she didn't embarrass herself.

"Thank you for walking with me. I'll run from here. Where I'm staying isn't far."

"My pleasure, enjoy the rest of your Sunday," he said. She waved and jogged off.

CHAPTER NINE

Bliss scowled at his crew as he watched them unsuspected from the large mouth of hangar one. He shook his head. They would never figure out the problem with hovercraft Seventy-Three at this rate. He sighed, plucking the toothpick from his mouth. He scrubbed a hand over his clean-shaven face. He was amazed that he was able to restrain from choking every one of his eight-man crew.

Footsteps echoed in the distance. A slap on the back made him curse, and he turned to face Shots in his khaki uniform. It was clear Shots wasn't getting dirty today or he'd have his fatigues on like Bliss.

"When are you gonna tell them the problem is a power supply in the junction box?" asked Shots.

"Never. This is a learning exercise," Bliss replied with a half-smile.

"How so?" Shots asked.

"Let's say common sense is running low with my crew today."

"So you're getting even with them for not following procedures. Right?"

"Maybe. No need to micromanage. They're moving along at a good pace. They just have to keep troubleshooting."

"A good pace." Shots laughed, sincerely amused.

"They've been at it for three hours. At most, it should've taken one."

He gave an indifferent shrug. "I was waiting for one of them to come to their senses and ask me if there was a better way to find the problem. Alas, that hasn't happened yet," Bliss said, looking dejected. Then he smiled wickedly.

"See that, right there?" Shots pointed at the smile on his face. "That's why I'm glad I changed jobs and became a craftmaster. That way, I didn't have to work for you anymore. Being your engineer for a year was a year too long."

"Nice try. Every engineer wants to be a craftmaster. Hell, everyone who works at the unit wants to drive hovercrafts or they wouldn't transfer here."

Shots shook his head. "I can't watch this. It brings back painful memories." Shots slapped him on the back once again and then got very serious. "Phillips said there was something I needed to know. Spill."

Bliss placed the toothpick back in his mouth, rolling it to the other side. He stared up at the clear sky. "It's Rose. She's moving for Oregon after the baby comes."

Shots was visibly deflated. It seemed as if he'd been punched in the gut. *Yep, something was going on.* Bliss didn't think Shots was aware of it, however. He and Shots were of the same mind on the topic of relationships. They were nothing but drama. Deployments placed too much strain on relationships.

"I think Chapman has something to do with it. Saw some bruises on her wrist. I tried to talk to her about them. I don't know if I can stay out of it, even if Rose wants me to. I don't want anything happening to the baby."

Shots's face went ugly, and his voice was a choked whisper. "Don't worry. I'll take care of that son of a bitch."

He chewed his toothpick. "You've put in sixteen years, retirement is around the corner. None of us need to throw it way for Chapman."

Shots clenched his jaw. "You're right. It's Rose though, we have to do something."

"What do you have in mind?"

"Oh, it's been a while since I've messed with anyone at work, so I'll have to think about it. But a lock box comes to mind. Maybe I'll lock him in one for about an hour and let him sweat his ass off on the apron while he repents for his misdeeds."

"I like the way you think. Maybe I'll find a nice sledge-hammer or some metal to pound on it. See if I can get it ringing real good."

"Chapman will be deaf for a week," Shots snickered, sounding way too pleased.

They both fell silent. Nine years ago, Bliss arrived at the unit and walked onto the apron to work on hovercraft Fifty-Six when out popped Shots, nosy as ever. Wanting to size up the competition. They were both known in the navy engineering community for being outstanding engineers. If there were egos involved, Bliss and Shots would have clashed, but that was not part of his personality. He'd seen too much testosterone slung around at WTF to want any part of it. He opened himself up to Shots right away, and before he knew it, they were coming to each other every time one of them had a problem with their respective crafts. There had been many late hours working on each other's craft to meet inspection. Bliss had ranked up as a chief two years before Shots and Shots became his engineer. It was a tough year on their friendship. Shots having to take orders from him took a stab to his pride, but they survived. Shots made chief and abandoned Bliss to head to Coronado for craftmaster school. Again, they were on equal footing, and they always watched each other's back. It was a good feeling.

"What time you heading out today?"

"Early," Bliss said.

"Peace out, my brother. See you later. I have paperwork to do," Shots said.

He watched Shots stroll out of the hangar toward the office buildings. Some of the maintenance guys in the hangar were picking up their tools and putting them away. The commotion caused him to stir. He glanced at his watch. It was almost lunch. He walked out to the apron and saw his loadmaster, Owns, crawling out from the engine tunnel covered in dirt and sweat. It had to be ninety degrees out on the craft. He finally decided to have mercy on his crew.

He approached, and his men murmured something about not getting readings on Engine Three. Their backs were to him. He stopped and stood behind Owns, not making a sound. Folding his arms across his chest, he waited for one of them to notice his presence. But after watching them for a while, he couldn't take it anymore.

"Have you checked the power supply?" he finally said.

His crew turned, and their mouths went slack. Sweat dripped off their brows.

"Why didn't you say something sooner?" Owns complained.

"If you used the manual, you would know what to check and in what order," he replied, pointing to the nametag shining on his chest. He wagged his finger under the nametag. "What does it say?"

"Chief Bliss," Owns replied.

"That's right. I don't say shit unless I already know the answer. So when I talk, learn to listen."

His crew was split down the middle. Half rolled their eyes at his arrogance while the other half clenched their jaws and cursed him with their eyes. He had an uncanny ability to be right when it came to hovercrafts. His crew might not like him, but they would do what he said and respected him.

Light streamed into the bedroom. *What the hell time is it?* Running a hand through her tangled hair, River glanced at the clock on the nightstand. It was noon. She rubbed her eyes and threw back the covers to lumber downstairs. This whole staying-up-all-night-and-sleeping-half-the-day thing was going to take some getting used to. She fixed coffee and leaned against the counter praying it brewed at top speed. Five hours before she had to be at work. She'd made some pretty crazy decisions the last few days and yet she didn't regret any of them thus far. Mathew would be impressed; hell, she was impress. She'd went out, met some interesting people, and had a great run with some funny guys. It had almost felt like Mathew was there cheering her on as she challenged the group of guys to step up. She chuckled to herself as the memory of Logston and Phillips panting and groaning.

She poured a cup of coffee and made her way to the sliding glass door leading to Mathew's back porch. He had a cute backyard with a three-foot flowerbed that was curved to outline a small patch of grass with one lone maple tree in the center of it. There was a decent-sized fishpond in the corner with a waterfall. There were four fish of some kind. When she feed them the first time, three fished had jumped out of the water and into the grass. She'd shrieked and shoved them back in. Mathew had never told her about any fish. Three were already dead and floating on top of the water when she arrived.

She sat on the grass next to the pond and watch her fish friends come up to greet her. She grabbed the food she'd found in the garage and tossed it into the water. They swam around, gobbling up the pieces. She'd named them Patch, Sam, Thing One, and Thing Two. Taking a sip of her coffee, she looked back at Mathew's house. She'd been here for over a week, and it didn't feel so foreign anymore. The house was open and inviting. She smiled. She liked it and it reminded her of

Mathew.

She thought about all the manuscripts she could be read-ing if she wanted to, but she shook the thought away. She wouldn't feel guilty about taking all her vacation days. Hell, she had forty-five days on the books. She wasn't even tech-nically on a leave of absence yet. She was burning up her vacation days. Not wanting to let guilt grip her, she thought about going to the farmer's market she'd see near WTF. She could use some food in the house, so why not try some-thing new? It would be a nice change to throw on a summer dress and get some sun on her white legs. "You know what, guys?" she said to the fish. "I'm going to the market." Little O mouths popped up at her. "Sorry you can't come. Maybe I can find something different for you to eat." She threw another round of food for them. She sat there a while longer, watching the fish eat, breathing in the fresh air. Yes, she could get used to this.

CHAPTER TEN

River went cross-eyed at the drink cheat sheet she'd typed up on Sunday. She prayed it would be a slow Monday night because Sarah was finally throwing her to the wolves. River was being pushed to mix and serve drinks tonight. She kept her anger at a low simmer. She had only a few hours to train with Chrissie. *Deep breath in . . . slow breath out. I should look at the bright side. I could be cleaning the tables.* The thought resonated inside her, and she felt tension ease.

"I'll take a Seven and Seven, sweet thing," said an old gentleman as he stepped up to the bar.

She swallowed. "Seven and Seven, coming right up," she said in the syrupy-sweet voice that made her want to stab her vocal cords.

Doubling back to the liquor shelf, she glanced at the bottle labels and spotted one on the second shelf. Seagram's Seven whiskey. That had to be it. She snatched the bottle, turned, and ran smack into Sarah. The impact caused her to stumble back. The bottle broke free from her fingers and shattered on the floor.

"Watch out," Sarah snarled. "Great, what a mess. Clean it up before I get cut." Sarah hurried back to the other end of the bar, mixing a cocktail for a guy who was staring at her boobs.

River looked apologetically at the old man. "I'm so sorry. You're going to have to order from her." She pointed to Sarah. She couldn't believe how pitiful she sounded just then.

"It's okay. I'm not going anywhere," said the man, pulling out a barstool to take a seat.

He was going to wait for her to finish his order. To her, it was an unexpected kindness in this stressful evening.

"Okay, give me ten minutes and I'll have your drink ready."

"No rush. I got all night."

She rushed down the hall to the storage room. When she got there, she grabbed a dustpan, broom, and a mop. As she hurried back to the bar and turned the corner, she broke hard right to avoid a mass of lean muscle blocking her path.

"Man, can someone cut me some slack?" she grumbled, ignoring the body in her path. She didn't make eye contact with Bliss, feeling awkward after their chance meeting on the beach yesterday morning. She didn't know if he wanted to be friends or more than friends. Thing was, it didn't seem right. He was her boss, and she was here to figure out how to find closure with Mathew's death. Getting involved with Bliss when she wasn't planning on staying around didn't seem fair. Their competitive run had been exhilarating—she couldn't remember the last time she'd had so much fun— but she didn't think it should happen again unless it was as friends.

She felt his eyes on her, but she kept working. A customer was waiting for her. Swiftly, she set the items down and bent to pick up the rubber mat. As her fingers wrapped around the edge, Bliss ordered her out of the way.

"Let me do that," he said in a rough tone, taking the mat from her.

Was he trying to be nice or just bossy? It was hard to tell. She decided it didn't really matter to her what his motive was. She could use the help. He didn't have to tell her twice.

Once more, she bustled down the hall to get a new bottle of Seagram's. When she came back, Bliss set the mat aside with his back to her and began to clean up the glass, his black fitted t-shirt and faded blue jeans hugging him nicely as he worked.

He stood as she passed, giving her room. Her breasts skimmed his back, and her heart thumped erratically at the friction. This man made her feel vulnerable, exposed. Moving away from him, she stared at her drink sheet. She didn't know what just happened, but she wasn't ready to figure it out.

Glass, scoop of ice, Seagram's, pour one–two–three seconds, 7-Up, pour to fill. River stared at the glass in delight, a smile tipping the corners of her mouth. That wasn't so bad. She placed the drink in front of the man who had been patiently waiting.

"Thanks," said the man, placing some money on the counter.

"It's on the house," she said. He smiled and gave her a wink.

Suddenly, the light from the bar was eclipsed. Bliss scowled at her. "Really?"

His breath skimmed her cheek. She swallowed hard and gave him a weak smile. "Take it out of my pay," she said, as a warm, silky tension wrapped around her middle when her eyes locked with his.

"And the bottle you dropped. I'll take that as well."

The warm, silky feeling vanished, and all she could do was glare at him. "Knock yourself out," she snapped, moving down the bar to help another customer. That was it. She was going to ignore him. Yep, most definitely the boss. Dropping the bottle had been an accident, and Sarah was partially responsible when she'd bumped into her.

Bliss disappeared with the trashcan and the mop a few moments later. She prayed he wouldn't come back, even if he did help her with the mess. Her nervousness was already getting the better of her. Taking in a breath, she pointed to a tall blue-eyed dream. What the heck was this? Handsome Men R Us? This one looked familiar. Recognition hit like the sky was falling. The run yesterday. Both men had been with Bliss.

"Can I get you a drink?" she said, placing her hands on the bar.

Bliss settled himself behind the bar like usual. Keeping an eye on his customers. He folded his arms across his chest when Shots and Logston took a seat at the bar and began drool over River. Well, that wasn't true only Logston was drooling.

"I'll take a Bloody Mary," Shots said, resting his elbows on the bar top.

"And I'll have a Coors. Please." Logston stared at River, all dreamy-eyed.

She smiled at them. "Coming right up," she chimed.

"Hey there, sexy. How was work?" Sarah said in a seductive voice to Shots.

He sagged on the stool. "Good, work was good. Same old shit, different day. The unit is going to hell, and the captain is driving the craft."

River carefully placed the drink in front of him to avoid being noticed by Sarah. Bliss could see their new working relationship was out of sight, out of mind.

"Why haven't you come to see me?" Sarah flipped her hair over her shoulder and pouted at him.

Bliss noted River leaning back and watching their exchange. *"Workups."*

"Oh hell, when do you deploy?"

"Hey there, Freddy Krueger. Nice of you to notice me," Logston butted in, irritated.

Sarah rolled her eyes and focused her attention on Shots.

"Can I get a drink down here, or do I have to serve myself?" asked an impatient young man. He banged the counter with his fist.

Sarah growled and walked off.

Shots took a sip. "So, how's work? The boss treating you okay?" he asked, hastily swallowing his drink. The liquid went down the wrong pipe, and he coughed and choked. Logston slapped a meaty hand on his back, causing the drink to come out his nose. Bliss grabbed a few napkins seeing a mix of Bloody Marry and tears running down his face, shoving them into a hand.

A light flashed, and Bliss turned to see Logston holding up his phone and laughing. "You're a bitch, you know that, right?" Shots said as he wiped his face dry.

"Call me what you will. This is going on the internet," Logston replied.

When Shots recovered from his coughing fit, he turned to River. She was looking at him, concern shadowing her face. "Too much pepper . . ." he rasped out. "Dial it down one shake, okay?" He gave her a thumbs-up. She visibly melted with relief, and she nodded. Bliss grumbled. River respond to everyone better than him. It was starting to piss him off.

"As I was saying . . . how's work?" Shots continued.

River glanced at Bliss, then said, "Is that a loaded question?"

Shots shrugged. "It can be if you want it to—but no, it's not intended that way."

"It's peachy," she said, flashing a fake smile. It made Shots chuckle. He lifted the glass to his lips once again and downed the drink prepared this time for the spice of it. Seconds later it was gone.

Shots tapped his glass on the counter. "Another drink, please," he said.

She jumped into action, pouring him another drink.

Logston got up and strolled over to the jukebox. A minute later, the sound of Tim McGraw's "Truck Yeah" bounced off the walls. Logston snapped his fingers and did an air guitar with his leg outstretched.

Bliss's chest ached at the sight of his friend. The leg air guitar was something Wagner did when he was in a good mood and was ready to mess around and blow off steam. He missed his friend. Always the life of the party. One time, Wagner hopped up on stage with Phillips and played the drums like a champ and sang like a mad man. They had all laughed at him. He wasn't afraid to throw himself into the moment, even if it was making a fool of himself. Wagner never apologized for being himself. It had been one of the nicest changes to the group, as Wagner always kept things light.

Logston plopped down on the seat and puffed his chest out and then ran a hand over his bald head. Bliss knew he was going to put the moves on River.

River settled another drink in front of Shots. "Thanks, beautiful, just keep them coming," Shots said.

"Having a binge night or what?" Bliss asked, tearing his eyes away from Logston.

"Maybe, maybe not. Don't think it really counts when there is tomato juice involved and a stick of celery."

River had a confused look on her face. Shots gave her a wink. The lines around her mouth softened. "Are you three good friends?" she asked, "You were there at the beach yesterday."

"I claim them both as my friends . . . on occasions," Bliss said, peering at the other end of the bar. Sarah was slapping a hand away before it reached her breasts, then moved on to the next customer without skipping a beat. She was a pain in more ways than one, but she could hold her own in a room full of grabby men.

"Yes, we work together over at the Hovercraft Unit, just

on the other side of Camp Pendleton," Shots responded.

"But you're navy." She tipped her head toward Bliss. "What are navy boys doing over there? It's marine territory."

"Not all, beautiful. Have you been on the 805 freeway, past the large concrete wall that reads, 'Honor, Courage, Commitment, and Go NAVY'?"

She wrinkled her nose at him, and took the order of a young man who stepped up next to Shots.

"How's it going, Chief?" the young man said to Bliss. "I'll take a Coors Light." It was Jones, an engineer and part of Chapman's crew. Bliss ignored him.

Shots shook Jones's hand. "Did you get your craft running?" Shots asked.

"I wish," Jones said, taking the Coors River held out to him.

"That will be two bucks," said River.

"Put it on my tab," ordered Shots.

"Thanks, Chief. See you around." Jones strolled off to mingle with a group sitting on the other side of the bar.

"Did you have to be an ass to the poor guy? It's not his fault he has to work for a scumbag," he complained to Bliss.

"Guilty by association."

"Nice, real nice." Shots ran a hand through his hair.

River tucked a strand of hair behind an ear. "You were telling me about the wall."

"Oh, right." Shots smiled, pleased she was interested. Logston must have sensed the same thing because he jumped in and took over the conversation.

"On the other side of that concrete wall are about forty hovercraft. We just call them 'craft,'" Logston announced proudly.

She folded her arms under her breasts with her mouth in a small O. "Do you fly them . . . or drive them?"

"The last one," Bliss answered, staring at Logston who

seemed unfazed.

"Can I come see one?" she blurted out before her hand flew to her mouth, her eyes wide.

"Sure, I'd love to show you the unit. How about tomorrow around noon, before your work shift? I'll pick you up here," Logston offered, sounding much too eager.

Bliss clenched his jaw, body as taut as a wire about to snap. River stared at the ground, biting the right corner of her lip, and her cheeks were coloring. On the other side of her mouth was the beginning of a smile.

Unexpectedly, she glanced at Bliss and smiled radiantly. "Yes. I'd love to check it out." Bliss met her gaze dead-on. She tore her eyes from him and continued talking to Logston. "I've seen them in pictures but never up close. It would be a once-in-a-lifetime experience," she said, blasting Logston with a genuine smile.

Bliss fought the urge to reach over the counter and strangle Logston just long enough to see him turn red and see his eyes bulge a little.

CHAPTER ELEVEN

Bliss glanced at his watch. Chapman had been in the large metal parts container for about forty-five minutes now, and boy was he pissed. The guy hadn't stopped yelling and banging from within the belly of the box. Thankfully, the constant pounding of waves from the other side of the unit drowned him out.

He had to give it to Shots. The way he'd conned Chapman onto the apron and into the box, and then slipping out and locking Chapman in was pure genius.

Thoughts of Rose swirled through his head. She would go berserk if she found out about what they'd done. She wouldn't find out though. Chapman was smart enough to keep his mouth shut, especially with the dirt he had on him.

He took a bite of his sandwich, trying to enjoy his lunch, but Chapman's constant banging was a bit distracting. He thought of the bruises on Rose's wrists and clenched his fist. Mustard and mayo dribbled from between his fingers, and he swore, setting his sandwich down hastily. He yanked a handkerchief from the back pocket of his khakis and quickly cleaned his hand while scanning the apron. Two Navy officers were laughing as they made their way to a blue Toyota.

He glanced at his watch once more. Fifty-five minutes. He packed up his ruined lunch and made his way over to the box. He was ready for this to be done. He knew Rose was a big girl, but he had no tolerance for Chapman messing with his family. Chapman had to pay for that.

As he leisurely strolled across the concrete apron to throw away his trash, he thought about Logston and how he would be arriving with River any minute now for the tour. He grumbled, irritated that Logston had been the first to ask her to the unit. He had been planning to do the same. That was if she ever stopped lifting her chin every time she looked his way. It was both annoying and intriguing.

He rolled to a stop in front of the container and shoved a toothpick into the corner of his mouth. He crossed his arms over his chest, glancing over his shoulder one last time. There was no one here—just him, Chapman, and the hammering sounds of the waves against the shore. The booming sounds continued to drown out Chapman's angry cries, as well as drown out what would come next.

He uncrossed his arms and walked over to the rock Shots had so kindly left behind for him. It was a white smooth stone bigger than two fists. He held its weight, took a breath, and stepped up to the crack of the door.

He tapped the rock on the door. The cries of Chapman's angry, hoarse voice ceased to deep gasps of air.

"How's it going in there?"

Chapman said nothing.

"I'll tell you this one time and one time only." He slammed the rock into the container as hard as he could, causing an ear-piercing sound to echo within the box. Chapman growled loudly.

He gave Chapman time to regain some of his hearing.

"You stay away from my sister. I see another bruise on her body, and I'll kill you in your sleep."

The seconds ticked by. He thought Chapman hadn't heard him, but then Chapman shouted, "Fuck you."

"Wrong answer." Rage filled him. A rage that flowed from the brotherly bond he held with his sister and his unborn nephew. A rage that would see both protected at all costs. He slammed the rock against the container with all his might. He could feel the metal vibrate beneath his palms. Chapman cried out, but Bliss wouldn't yield—not for this man. He slammed the rock against the metal over and over until he was dripping with sweat. When the last of his rage had been spent, the rock slipped from his fingertips and thumped to the ground. He lifted the latch and opened the door.

Chapman lay on the ground with his hands covering his ears. His body trembled and was drenched in sweat. He had stripped off the top half of his uniform.

A stab of pain shot through Bliss's chest, not for hurting this sad excuse of a man, but for the shame he had just brought to his fellow Goat Locker brother. He was a chief, and his actions on this day were anything but the respectable actions of a chief. They were the actions of a scared, desperate man losing control. Bliss shook his head as if he could erase it from his mind. He turned his back on Chapman and walked away. A desperate man was a man to be feared.

CHAPTER TWELVE

River fidgeted with the front pocket of her jeans as she bathed in the heat of the sun. A soft breeze played through her loose hair, but she was practically melting. The crashing waves masked the buzzing chatter in her head. *This isn't a date, is it? No.* She tugged at the neck of her rose-colored blouse and rubbed her sneakers against each other. She hadn't been on a date in almost five years and hadn't been in anything that resembled a relationship since college. Guys, dating, it was never a priority to her. She'd been happy just doing her own thing figuring herself out.

She had warmed up to Logston . . . at least enough to agree to this outing. Yes, he was pompous, but based on their interactions, she could tell he was harmless. Weirdly, she was excited and nervous about seeing him. It felt weird because she hadn't been excited about anything in a long time. *Why did I say yes to this? Some guy I hardly know asks me to go see a hovercraft and suddenly I act like a five year old.*

The sound of loud exhaust pipes snapped her back from her negative self-talk. She spotted a lifted black Ford 250 as it slowed and turned into the WTF parking lot. She sucked in a breath. She'd wanted to do this since Mathew first showed her a picture of a hovercraft after his first deployment years ago. He'd raved about them and how it felt to ride on one.

A memory of Mathew surfaced—him laughing and talking about what he'd done with his buddies overseas. Her chest ached. Some of her excitement dwindled and she felt cold. But Mathew would be happy to know she was doing something new. She could hear his voice in her head: *Suck it up, River. Take a risk.*

The black truck rolled to a stop in front of her.

"Hey there, sweet cheeks, want to take a ride with your Romeo?" Logston was wagging his brows up and down, dark eyes glowing with enthusiasm.

She gave him five points for his effort to be smooth.

He leaned over and popped the door open for her. She tentatively approached his small monster truck. Logston wore a blue digital camouflage uniform, his hat riding shotgun in the passenger seat. Her heart sped up a little. A man in uniform never failed to take her breath away, warranted or not. It stood for bravery, determination, and honor.

"How do I get in . . .?" She looked around, but there was no sidestep.

Logston chuckled. "You have three options. One, grab the oh-shit handle and push off from the corner of the doorframe hard with your foot. Two, get a running start and jump in, or three, I can walk over there and lift you up."

She gawked at him.

"Tick tock, sweet cheeks, my lunch doesn't last forever." He leaned back in his seat, his arm resting on the driver-side window.

Not seeing how one could push off the doorframe and actually reach the oh-shit handle, she sighed and swore under her breath. She didn't want Logston to help her either. He clearly had the wrong idea about what was happening between them—absolutely nothing. She was taking the opportunity to be closer to Mathew, by sharing an experience in this small way. She would go with the run-and-leap option. She walked back a few yards, feeling silly about her choice.

"All right, get some," he said, clapping his hands.

She sprinted for the truck, and on the last second before impact, she jumped as high as she could and launched herself into the truck. With an unattractive belly flop into the seat, she was in.

"Woo-wee, I knew you would be fun to have around. That was as graceful as a ballerina with two broken legs. I should've gotten that on camera and saved it for YouTube."

"Thanks," she said, righting herself, blushing to the roots of her hair.

In no time they were at the main gate to Camp Pendleton. Logston flashed his military ID at the guard. He was greeted with "Welcome, Chief," and then they cruised onto the base. River felt the butterflies flutter in her stomach.

She was pressed to the door with the window down. Her gaze bounced from houses to buildings, a gas station, a McDonald's, a new hospital, a NEX, and a commissary . . .

"That's a big NEX. It looks new," she said.

"Sure is." Logston studied her a moment. "You familiar with the military life?"

She thought for a second. Did she want to answer that? She shrugged, why not? Everyone could use some backstory. "Yes. My mother is in the navy."

"Really? Interesting. So you're familiar with deployments and moving." Logston sounded pleased for some reason.

She wrinkled her nose. Maybe the backstory wasn't a good idea. But she had to start somewhere eventually. "Yes, we moved a few times when I was little. My mom was an instructor at A-school in Great Lakes for three years, and then she went to a ship in San Diego at 32st . . . for about five years, then we moved to Boise where she recruited and I graduated high school and went to college."

"I didn't hear anything about a father in the mix."

She blew out a breath. "He left when I was little after my mom came back from a deployment. My mother isn't nice. They fought, he left, the end. I prefer to stay away from that kind of life now that I have a choice."

He frowned at that and she almost laughed.

They drove down a small hill to a traffic light where they turned left.

"How big is this place?" she asked, downshifting into tourist mode.

"Big."

"Really? That's all you got for me? What kind of tour is this?"

He looked at her with a curl-your-toes kind of smile, even with the scar. "Sweet cheeks, I'm a navy chief, not a marine. And the tour is of the hovercraft unit, not Pendleton."

Okay, so he had her there. She would let him off the hook. Yet, she deducted a brownie point. She felt him studying her, and she tried not to squirm.

"What do you think of WTF?" he asked, cool and collected.

She didn't know what to say because she didn't have an opinion yet.

"It gets busy, doesn't it?"

"Sure does. Anytime Phillips gets up on that stage or even when he's just in the building, the girls swarm to him."

"He's a good singer."

They passed a group of houses on the left as the road curved. The houses were large, but with no backyard and only small porches. They came to another light. A bridge stretched over the freeway, and she saw the concrete wall Shots had been talking about yesterday. *Honor, Courage, Commitment, Go Navy.*

Logston made a left turn, and his truck climbed over the bridge with little effort. They rolled up next to the guard shack. Once more, he handed his ID over to the guard who then waved him in.

She now vibrated with anticipation. Logston pulled past the guard station and made a quick left. They passed between a small hill and the concrete wall with the writing. Just ahead, a large concrete slab stretched out farther than three football fields. Her jaw dropped. There were three rows of hovercraft, the size of a small single-story house.

Logston parked next to what looked like an office building. After turning off the engine, he leaned forward to rest his arms over his steering wheel and stared at something in the distance. The energy he had been emitting evaporated. *What is he staring at?*

"Is everything okay?" she asked, wanting to get out of the truck.

"Let's go."

She unlatched the truck door and pushed it open, then peered down at the ground. *Great, now I'm going to face plant.* As she braced herself to shimmy down the seat, a large hand reached inside the truck and pushed a button under the dashboard. Her heart leaped into her throat.

Bliss stepped up in his khakis, offering his hand. Amber eyes roamed over her face. A toothpick rested in the corner of his mouth.

"Did I scare you?"

She tried to disguise her annoyance but was unsuccessful. "Where the heck did you come from?" she demanded, sweeping her gaze around. There had been no one when they drove up.

She leaned out and looked down. There was now a footstep she could use to get down from the truck. She turned to Logston, hair tumbling over her shoulder. "You're an ass," she said.

"A guy has to have a little fun now and then," Logston said, hopping out of the cab.

"Yeah, sure, whatever," she said, aggravated and slightly amused. She held back a smile. She knew better than to show

Logston she found him entertaining. It would be an open invitation to heckle her all the time. He reminded her of Mathew.

When she took Bliss's hand, an electric pulse zipped up her arm. There was something so irritating about him. His maddening arrogance, his soothing manner . . . he was disconcerting. Her attraction to him was undeniable, no matter how she questioned her feelings.

The electric charge settled in her chest, speeding her heart rate to the pace of a sprinting Olympian running for a gold medal. She placed a foot on the sidestep and he helped her step down. He didn't release her hand. She didn't know why, but she had the feeling this was out of character for him—tenderness.

A throaty sound came from behind her, and Bliss released her hand. "Are we going to do this, or should I just leave you with him?" Logston snickered.

"No . . . no . . . I'm ready," she stammered.

Bliss didn't say a word, merely fell into step beside Logston with his hands in his pockets.

"Where to start? How about with a hovercraft, and then I'll show you around the unit?"

"That would be great." She tried her best to gain composure. "How long have you worked with hovercraft?"

"About sixteen years."

"Wow. Have you ever worked on a ship?"

Bliss chuckled beside Logston, who had stiffened for a moment.

"She really knows how to cut your heart out," said Bliss, smiling.

"Shut up," Logston glared at him. "I've never been stationed on a ship. Went to boot camp and A-school and got sent here. Been here ever since."

"Oh." River fidgeted with her jeans pockets, feeling uneasy. Why was she asking personal questions? That wasn't what she was here for.

The gunmetal gray craft had "73" painted on it in black. Logston walked her up a ramp that seemed to be the mouth of the craft. Bliss stayed behind as Logston launched into tour-guide mode.

But River was hardly listening. "There's nothing like riding these babies," Mathew would say with that crooked smile of his.

"An LCAC is a Landing Craft Air Cushion vehicle otherwise known as a 'hovercraft.'" Logston finger-quoted the air. "They're supported by high-volume air. The air is ejected against the surface of the water or land by four lift fans." As Logston told her details about the craft, Mathew was suddenly standing there, watching her smiling, hands crossed over his chest, sleek brows wagging up and down to emphasize what Logston was saying. She blinked, thinking Mathew would disappear, but he was still there. A knot formed in her throat.

"The air is then contained by one of two types of rubber skirts: one being a legacy, and the other being a deep skirt. The deep skirt is the larger of the two. These skirts allow the craft to hover six to eight feet in the air. Though the craft hovers, they're not considered an aircraft. However, all our drivers have flight status."

Logston walked the deck. She was motionless, afraid Mathew would disappear. He moved toward her, reached out and took her hand, encouraging her to touch the heated metal warmed by the sun. She couldn't pull her eyes away from Mathew. She just smiled, wanting him to be real, wanting him to be there with her. A single tear rolled down her cheek and on to the metal deck. Mathew winked and then he was gone.

Logston approached a door and unlocked it. He swung it open and gestured for her to step inside. It took several breaths before she could move. She wiped another tear away and caught Bliss watching her with a concerned expression.

"This is the starboard cabin or cockpit."

The moment she stepped into the small, cramped space, she inhaled that heady scent of old metal, grease, oil, and a hint of paint. She closed her eyes and smiled. It was as though Mathew embraced her. A stabbing pain caused her heart to stop. Another piece of her was dying. She grabbed the metal ladder that led to where she assumed the crew sat and steadied herself.

Logston continued from behind her, unaware of her sudden weakness. "The concept design of a present-day LCAC was introduced in the 1970s, but the first delivery to the US Navy was in 1984, and initial operational capability was achieved in 1986. Approval for production was in 1987. A craft has a minimum crew of five: a craftmaster, who pilots the craft, an engineer, a navigator, and two loadmasters. According to the United States Marine Corps, these craft can access 70 percent of the world's coastline, as opposed to about 15 percent for conventional landing craft such as an LCU, though the craft has more difficulty in rough seas than a conventional LCU."

After a few deep breaths, she was in control of herself. Logston nudged her in the side.

"Climb up into a seat. Have a look."

"Really? It's okay?" she asked, gripping the ladder and pulling herself up.

"Go for it. Everyone wants to sit in the craftmaster's seat."

She climbed the ladder and was in the driver's seat. Wow. It seemed pretty high, and it wasn't even hovering yet. Her stomach rolled abruptly. The thought of being out on rough seas in this small space would make her sick for sure. She felt sorry for anyone who had to hitch a ride on one of these things. And to think Mathew had loved it. She wondered where they put passengers.

"There are only ninety-one of these craft in the entire US Navy. They're used for transporting weapons systems, equipment, cargo, and the marine air-ground task force from ships to shore and across the beach. A single craft weights eighty-seven-point-two tons and can carry sixty to seventy-five tons. This translates to approximately one tank or eight Humvees. Top speed is roughly seventy knots with no payload."

Her smile was back. Logston sure knew his stuff. "This is amazing."

"You should see us cruising San Diego Harbor by Seaport Village at dusk. We get in there kicking up a spray off the skirt something fierce. Next thing you know, we're getting a call over the radio asking if the craft is okay. People think the craft is on fire when the light hits the spray just right."

"I'm sure it's magnificent. Where do people sit when they ride on the craft?"

"Come on, that's on the other side. But most of the time, the guys ride in what they loaded on board. Tank, Hummer, what-ever."

She climbed out of the cockpit and moved to the other side of the craft. Logston once more unlocked a heavy metal door. When it swung open, she peered inside. It was just as small as the cockpit with the exception of two top and lower rows of seats. The space had no windows. *Dear God, who would like sitting in that?*

"Don't people get sick when they sit in here?"

"All the time, sweet cheeks. That's why it can be hosed out." Logston ran a hand over his head, amused.

"Well, that's it, want to see my office?"

"Sure."

They walked down the ramp and off the craft. River turned back for one last look. Mathew was there again leaning against the door to the cockpit with his crooked smile that was just for her. She blew out a breath and followed Logston. The tour had been great, but when she met Bliss's cold stare and turned-down lips, she frowned back at him. Some of her enthusiasm waned. Logston walked past him, taking her by the elbow. She swore she heard Bliss growl as Logston hurried her away. After a minute or two of walking, she glanced over her shoulder. He looked displeased, and then he turned, walking off in the opposite direction.

CHAPTER THIRTEEN

Logston walked her in the direction of a large hangar, but River was distracted. The image of Mathew was burned in her memory. He was so real, she could almost reach out and touch him.

They approached two doors that were marked with a large One and Two. A gigantic blue metal structure hovered over one of the craft with monster-size tires.

"What's that?" she asked, amazed.

"What?" Logston stopped.

"That blue thing."

"A bigfoot."

"What's it used for?"

He grinned, walking her through the hangar, "The bigfoot lifts the craft and moves it." Then his eyes grew wide. "Watch out," he said as he pulled her to his side. He pointed to a pile of bones and . . . poop.

She gasped. "Gross."

"You're telling me. We have to clean that shit up—literal shit—at least once a week."

"What makes that mess?" She wrinkled her nose at the offending smell.

"The biggest fucking owl I've ever seen. It lives in the corner over there. You can't see him. But some of the guys on duty have seen him come out to hunt at night."

They made their way toward the office building. When she entered the office building, people buzzed past her, phones were ringing behind cubical walls, and laughter sounded from all corners of the building.

Her mouth dried, and her nerves started to vibrate under her skin, causing it to tighten. *Shit.* She'd been doing so go, not letting her triggers set off her anxiety. But she was already stressed being here with Logston, and with Bliss added to the mix, she hit saturation for the day.

"Where's the ladies' room?"

"The women's head is down the hall to the right."

"Thanks." She followed his directions and found the door. Quickly, she slipped inside and locked it. She washed her sweaty hands in the sink. After dampening a paper towel, she pressed it against her cheeks and neck, trying to cool her skin. She was so hot, and her heart was pounding. *An office full of men—seriously, why did I agree to see his office?* She let out a breath and noticed her reflection. *Why was it so easy to say yes to Logston? He did scare the shit out of me only a week ago? It was confusing. I will not cower, but overcome.*

Her face had red blotches, as well as her chest. She pressed a finger to her chest and a white dot appeared. *Great, just what I need. People will stare and ask me if I'm okay.* Happened every time her blood pressure climbed.

Running her fingers through her hair, she readied herself to leave. I can do this. After a few minutes, she unlocked the restroom door and stepped out into the hallway. As she turned the corner, she slammed into someone and staggered back. A hand shot out and clasped her forearm, helping her regain her footing.

"I'm so sorry. I didn't look."

When she looked up, her breath caught in her throat.

"No worries. I wasn't paying attention too. I was looking for someone," the man said, red-faced and hoarse.

She couldn't take her eyes off him. He looked like Mathew. He had the same brunette hair cropped close to his scalp, was the same height, and had a lean build. Even his eyes were a similar shade of green. If she'd seen the young man at a distance, she would have thought she was seeing a ghost.

There was a disconnected look in his eyes. It made her shudder. Trouble. She could feel it.

"Who are you looking for?" He looked her up and down for a second, and then pressed his thin lips together, saying nothing.

Next came a loud burst of deep laughter. They both looked in the direction of the sound. The young man's body flexed so tight the veins in his neck started to pop out. He pushed her aside and marched with purpose down the hall. She followed him at a safe distance.

The young man rounded the cubical wall and halted. She stayed out of sight.

"You pieces of shit," said the young man. "You two ever get near me again, and I'll have you in front of the captain."

Bliss was sitting on the edge of a desk talking to Shots who sat behind it, leaning way back in his desk chair. Logston was standing near the wall. She remained still and listened to the exchange.

Shots spoke first. "Ha. I'd like to see a slimy bottom feeder like you try it."

"I will," said the young man, getting louder.

Someone brushed her arm and she startled. It was a short man in khakis. He strolled passed her without a second glance. River straightened, realizing how silly she must look to passersby.

"You try it," Bliss sneered, "and I'll tell them what you

did. I might get reprimanded. But you'll go to jail."

The young man's ears turned bright red as he fisted his hands at his side. Just when she thought the young man was going to pop his top, he pivoted around and disappeared down the hall.

It all came rushing in on her—where she was, seeing Mathew, never seeing him again. Tears filled her eyes. She sniffled, unaware her nose had started to run. Then a bald head popped out from behind the corner.

"Hello, sweet cheeks. I knew you couldn't stay away from me for long. What's got you down?" Logston said.

"My nose? Allergies," she said. She stepped away from the wall.

Bliss walked around the corner with easy grace and took her by the elbow, leading her away from Logston. As they passed, Bliss shoved Logston's head back down.

"Stay here," he said to Logston in a calm voice. She could see he was anything but calm. His eyes were slits, and there were stress lines around his mouth. She was becoming familiar with them.

Shots and Logston's voices faded away behind her. Her gaze clung to Bliss. What was with him? She didn't need to be rescued. Embarrassment washed through her. Could he tell something had upset her? Did he pay more attention to her than she thought? Her heart sped up like a hummingbird. She was grateful. Maybe underneath all that male armor he was more compassionate than she realized.

He gently escorted her out the side of the building to a wide-open grassy area with one lone path to another building that read "Galley." He released her elbow. She wrapped her arms around her waist. His eyes were on her. She brushed a chunk of hair behind her ear and met his gaze, lifting her chin.

"Thank you," she said in a soft voice.

"Don't mention it."

She looked at the ground. *All these disturbingly handsome men trying to encroach on my life are affecting me more than I want to admit.* She glanced over her shoulder, thoughtful for a moment. *They are all sweet in their own way.*

"What was that about back there?" she asked, trying to pull the attention away from herself.

"Nothing you need be concerned with. Chapman wants to play with the big boys, but he's a toddler." He picked a leaf off a bush at his side. "I should ask you the same thing."

"What do you mean?"

He pointed at the door they exited. "What got you upset? And don't tell me you were sniffling because of allergies."

She could tell he really expected her to answer him. Well, he was in for a surprise. She wasn't at work, and she didn't have to tell him anything. Instantly, she hardened her heart. She wasn't ready to talk about Mathew, wasn't even sure she could. So she didn't, it was easier that way. Was that what she wanted, easy?

"In the bathroom or the office, I don't know, there was something that triggered my allergies. Now that I'm outside I should be fine."

He was silent, and that irritated her. She glanced at her watch; she had to be at work by two. She was working with Chrissie tonight since it was Sarah's night off.

"I'm sorry, but I have to get to work." She started to turn toward the office when Bliss caught her arm and stepped into her personal bubble. It was becoming a pattern with him. His male scent captured her attention—soap and a hint of grease.

"I'll take you. I haven't gone to lunch yet."

"But . . ."

He raised a brow and frowned at her.

"What about Logston?"

"Don't worry about him. Let him sweat."

꿎

Bliss fought a smile as River gawked at his Harley. The way she stood there with the sun shining off her hair and pale skin made him feel suddenly buoyant.

"You want me to ride on that . . . with you? I think I'll pass." She turned, but he quickly pulled her back.

"It'll be fine. I promise," he said. This retreating from him constantly was beginning to annoy him more than he cared to admit.

He let her go. He saddled the Harley and strapped on his helmet. Then he opened a leather saddlebag and pulled out a helmet for her. She stared at it warily and bit her lip. He watched with amusement as he read the expressions on her face. First there was doubt as she mulled over the situation. Then anxiety flitted through her eyes. Finally, the trademark lifting of her chin. After a few seconds, she grabbed the helmet from his hand. *Atta girl.* He found her determination to overcome challenges admirable. A determined spirit recognized a comrade. Perhaps he had something in common with her.

He was pleased with how things were progressing. Now she had no choice but to cozy up to him, and damned if that didn't cause his shaft to harden.

As he started his Harley, he straightened and pushed the kickstand back. He settled in the seat as it rumbled between his legs. *Power.* While he waited for her to get behind him, Bliss slipped on his orange vest with reflectors. She was smiling from ear to ear.

"Nice vest," she teased.

Bliss swore under his breath. "Have to wear one if I want Rose to get my life insurance if ever I get killed riding this thing. Military policy."

"And that's supposed to make me want to ride with you on this"—she waved her hand at the Harley—"death trap?"

"It's really not a trap. You'll fly right off."

She scowled at him, and he chuckled. "Don't have all day. Chrissie will be waiting for you."

With a heavy sigh, she swung a leg over, arranging herself on the small leather seat behind him. She leaned her weight toward him, but she didn't wrap her arms around his waist.

Shrugging, he slowly pulled out of his parking spot. Then he gassed it, forcing her to quickly lock her arms around him or fall off. He laughed to himself.

At first, she was stiff against his back, but then she slowly relaxed as they rode and he felt her mold against him nicely. His heart raced. As he pulled up to a traffic signal two blocks from WTF, he was overwhelmed with the urge to touch her. He reached down and placed his hand over hers. It was a small thing, but he needed it. He needed to see how she would respond.

As his hand rested on hers, he slowly caressed her fingers. Again, she stiffened and leaned away from him. He wanted to hold her tightly in place, but it wasn't what she wanted. He released her hand. A few seconds later, the light changed. He couldn't ignore the disappointment he felt.

He took off, tail pipes bellowing. She didn't grip his waist this time. Bliss tried to accept her rejection. He had never forced himself on anyone before. A few minutes went by and they arrived at WTF's parking lot. Chrissie was just about to unlock the door. She waved to them and went inside.

He stopped but didn't turn off his Harley. There was no point in rubbing the salt on his wounded ego.

River got off and returned the helmet in the leather bag. He kicked it into neutral and started to push the Harley backwards, preparing to take off, when he felt her hand on his arm.

"Thank you for the ride, it was . . . nice," she said, her cheeks coloring. Slowly, her soft fingers released his arm, and then she retreated into WTF. He watched her go. It was a start, but a start to what he wasn't sure.

River was the Energizer Bunny. She had helped Chrissie dust and clean the entire bar in two hours. She couldn't stop thinking about Bliss and the way he'd touched her hand. It had been so tender and perfectly sweet. It had caused her body to shudder with longing. He'd tried to put the moves on her. She chewed on her lip, deep in thought, when the knife she was using to cut lemons sliced into the side of her finger. She squeaked and dropped the knife and pressed the cut to her lips. *Pay attention.*

When she reached for the first-aid kit, she jumped when she was met by Chrissie, who was shaking her head, her arms crossed over her chest.

"You got it bad," Chrissie said, dark chocolate eyes filled with laughter.

River took a step back, her finger still in her mouth and found she couldn't fight the heat rushing to her cheeks. Carefully, she snatched the kit from behind Chrissie and opened the box to get a Band-Aid.

"What're you talking about?" she said.

"Oh, honey, I saw you two together."

River wrapped the Band-Aid around her bleeding finger. "Bliss and I? He was just giving me a ride back from the unit. Logston showed me the hovercraft."

"Ha. He never lets anyone near his Harley. One time, he caught me sitting on it in the alley. He almost popped that vein in his forehead, he was so angry."

River stared. She had been excited when he'd touched her hand, but the thought of him giving her special treatment made her uneasy. She wasn't anything special. Just a girl grieving for her brother the best way she knew how—by honoring his last wish to see his life here. *What was she thinking getting involved with her boss?*

Suddenly, the door swung open, and there was Rose, round and miserable looking. Her hand was on the curve of her lower back, counterbalancing the weight of her belly. She waddled over.

"Honey, you look like shit," Chrissie said.

"And hello to you too," Rose said to Chrissie in a grumpy tone.

River hurried out from behind the bar to help Rose to a chair. "Sit, take a break."

Rose was so small, and her belly was so round. There was no way for her to be comfortable with all that baby moving around inside her. She wrinkled her nose as if she were uncomfortable and slowly lowered herself into the chair. "Never thought I could get pooped just walking from the car to this place. I need a break."

"Why are you here? I thought Bliss banned you last week. I think he's worried you'll pop right here in the bar," Chrissie said, grabbing a cup full of ice and pouring some water into it. She handed Rose the cup.

"He did. But I'm bored at home. I'll work until my due date."

"When's that?" asked River.

"A few days from now."

"Really? You couldn't last at home?" said Chrissie, raising a brow. "Bliss is going to shit when he sees you here." She glanced at her watch. "Smoke break. Be on the patio when the MMI arrives."

"You're the biggest wimp ever. You always tuck tail and run," Rose complained to Chrissie's back. Chrissie held up a peace sign with her fingers and disappeared onto the patio.

River couldn't suppress a chuckle. Today it seemed simpler to be . . . happy. She was really starting to enjoy these people. It made the pain in her heart a little easier to handle, and for that, she was grateful.

"Rose, you should really go home. No one is here." River turned to the old, wrinkly marine vet sitting on a barstool in the corner. He'd ordered a shot of vodka. He took the shot and hadn't moved since. River swore he was holding the vodka in his mouth as though trying to make it last.

River grew concerned; Rose didn't look good. "Rose, do you want me to help you to the DAF room?"

"No. I need to talk to Bliss, but I want to lie down in the meantime—in the loft."

"I don't think the stairs are a good idea," she said.

"Do it or get out of my way."

She flinched. It reminded her of her mother's hard, demanding tone. It was a tone that could crush River's self-esteem in a second if she didn't armor up. She'd been a pleaser since she was a kid when it came to her mother, but when she left for college she left that behind as well.

She took Rose's arm and helped her out of the chair.

Tears pooled in Rose's eyes. "I'm so sorry. This kid is driving me crazy. If he doesn't come out soon, I may try to go in and get him."

The wall that instinctively went up to protect herself with Rose's outburst and crappie tone crumbled. "It's okay. I don't have a clue what you're going through, but I can imagine."

"No, you can't," Rose snapped again.

This time the tears rolled down Rose's cheeks, and her hand covered her mouth. "I'm a crazy woman. Please help me upstairs before I get any grumpier."

"No problem." Slowly, they made their way to the back of WTF.

"I'll be back in a few minutes. If you need something, Chrissie's on the patio," she said to the man at the bar.

The vet gave her a wink and a thumbs-up. Rose glanced

over to where the man was resting and waved.

"Hi, Sammy. You don't get too drunk now, you hear?" Rose said to him.

As they made slow progress down the hall, Rose said, "That's Sammy. He lives in the alley beside the bar. He comes in once in a while when he has money. Bliss takes pity on him and lets him shower so he doesn't stink the place up. He's nice."

To think of Bliss helping a homeless man made her feel a little squishy inside. It was a very kind thing to do. River was starting to understand that Bliss was a man who wanted to do the right thing. What made him hide his kindness from her or anyone?

As they reached the stairs, Rose groaned. "If these stairs don't make this kid want to come out, I don't know what will."

"Go slow, I'm behind you."

With a little push here and a little tug there, she and Rose were at his door in no time at all.

Rose was panting and groaning. She placed a hand on her belly. "These Braxton Hicks contractions suck. I'm so not looking forward to labor."

River didn't have a clue what Rose was talking about. Rose unlocked the door to the loft to reveal a hot, sweaty Bliss wearing black spandex shorts punching a body bag to death.

Bliss jabbed twice and spun with a roundhouse kick, landing it on the side of the bag. The intense look on his face would have been enough to frighten any opponent. River was hypnotized by the power and strength that radiated from him. Her core heated. She was fooling herself pretending she didn't find Bliss desirable. She wanted to run her fingers along every inch of his tight muscles.

"How did you sneak in?" she blurted out.

His intensity disappeared when he spotted his sister, only to be replaced with a worried look. He rushed over. "Are you okay? Did something happen? Is it the baby?" he questioned, taking Rose's arm.

Rose held up a hand. "I need to rest is all. Can I use your bed? I don't want to be alone."

He wrapped an arm around his sister's shoulder and ushered her over to his bed.

River couldn't help glancing around. Windows wrapped around the entire loft, flooding it with light. A few pieces of furniture were sprinkled about—TV, a recliner with holes in it, an end table next to it, and a king-sized bed across from what appeared to be a glowing white kitchen area. The open-ness of the loft made it seem empty.

She quickly followed them, just to check if Rose wanted any-thing before she went back downstairs. Slipping her thumbs into her front jeans pockets, she tried not to fidget.

Bliss gingerly helped Rose into his bed, tucking a pillow under her head, another between her knees, and a third be-tween her arms for her to hold. He reached for the covers at the bottom of the bed and pulled them over his sister. He stared at her with such concern and love.

River was struck with grief. Her grief was unpredict-able, overwhelming her from time to time over the simplest things, such as sibling love. Her chest twisted so tight the pain almost brought her to her knees.

"Thank you, Maddox," Rose said, her eyes fluttering closed.

It was too much—their love for one another. The wound in her heart, which had barely begun to mend, ripped open. She would never experience love like that again, and it was more than she could bear. She turned and hurried from the loft. Hot tears rolled down her cheeks. She didn't bother to wipe them away. It would be pointless. More would replace them.

River rushed behind the bar where she'd stashed her purse. Chrissie was back from her smoke break and was talking to Sammy, who seemed to have finally swallowed his vodka.

"I have to go. I can't work tonight. I'm sorry. Please tell Bliss and Rose when they come down."

"What? Bliss is upstairs? Weird, he always comes through the bar to go to the loft." Chrissie raised a thin brow at her.

"I have to go."

"You okay? Did Bliss yell at you? I'll kick his ass if he did. I don't have time to train someone else before Rose pops, and I'm so not working with Sarah every night."

"No, he didn't yell at me. Something came up. I'll see you tomorrow."

"Okay."

River heard the confusion in Chrissie's voice but kept moving. She was out the door and reached her rental car. She climbed in and shut herself away from the world. Deep breath in, deep breath out. *I've got this.*

More tears blurred her vision, and she blinked them away. But down her cheeks they continued to roll. *Mathew . . .* She sniffled as she started the car. Her eyes darted to the loft. Bliss was going to be pissed when he found out she was gone. She hoped he wouldn't fire her.

How many times would she drive these streets with blurry tears? She did her best, knowing her way around the windy back roads. All she wanted was to get home and curl up in bed.

Home. What did that mean? This wasn't her home; it was Mathew's home. The more she thought about it. She wasn't even sure if she knew what home felt like.

River drew in a ragged breath and parked the car in Mathew's driveway. Home had never been a place. Somewhere to sit and hide from the world . . . she searched her mind for the words, but it was her heart that answered. Home was a feeling of belonging, and her home had always been Mathew.

Hands shaking, she opened the door and stumbled out of the car, and she stopped. Who was she kidding? Mathew wasn't in that house. It was just stuff. Stuff she needed to get rid of. She tried to think about something else, something happier. She studied the house. What would it be like to see this house full of life, to see it filled with children and unconditional love? The thoughts didn't ease the stabbing in her heart. It heightened her pain.

Deep inside, she wanted so many things to be different. Things that had surfaced a little more every day since she'd arrived in California. But being here wasn't going to change anything. The closer her wants surfaced, the harder it became for her to function. She felt so raw.

Making her way into the house and feeling very tired, she went straight to bed. Tomorrow was a new day to face the sadness.

CHAPTER FOURTEEN

When Rose began to breathe deeply, Bliss knew she was asleep. Though he didn't know how because he'd been watching her belly for the past twenty minutes and it hadn't stopped moving. His nephew was going to keep her busy by the looks of him.

It hurt to think about not being part of his nephew's life. He didn't want to think about a life without Rose in it every single day. He wished things could be different, that he could find a way to protect her so she could safely remain nearby. He knew she was afraid of Chapman hurting her and her son. If she stayed, she would live in fear. Rose deserved to be happy. He wished she would get a restraining order or something.

Rising off the edge of the bed, he realized River had slipped away without him noticing. He'd been so distracted by Rose he hadn't even acknowledged her. He would have to make it up to her after he showered. He would get her some flowers. That was a sure way to make a woman smile. And he did want to see her smile. Every time she did, his heart skipped a beat and his cock turned rock hard. He went to the bathroom to take a cold shower.

Twenty minutes later, with Rose safely tucked away, he closed the door to his loft. He was glad she was here. After the stunt he and Shots pulled with Chapman, who knew what Chapman would do to retaliate?

As he strolled into the bar, eager to see River, he was blocked by Chrissie. Her ponytail swung as she jumped in his way, a hip pitched to the side. He scowled.

She poked him in the chest hard. "What did you do to River, boss man?"

He was confused. "What're you talking about? I didn't do anything to her," he said, backing away.

"Sure, that's why she took off about an hour ago. Leaving me here alone to deal with these pains in the butt." Chrissie pitched her hip in the direction of Phillips, Shots, and Logston who were sitting at the bar, beers in hand. His eyes narrowed as they all smiled sheepishly at him. *All of them together. Something's up.*

"She left? Where did she go?" He masked his disappointment in front of his friends.

"Hell if I know. She helped Rose upstairs, and the next thing I know, she flies out of here like a bat with the fires of hell nipping at her wings."

"Nice description," Phillips said in his smooth voice, giving Chrissie a wink and kissy lips.

She rolled her eyes. "Can you make them leave, please?"

He collected his desire to see River and stashed it deep inside himself. He had a business to run, which needed his full attention whether he wanted to give it or not. "Did they pay for their beer?" he asked.

Shots, Phillips, and Logston all frowned at him.

"They've paid."

"Then no. You have to put up with them just like any customer."

"You suck," said Chrissie. She walked over to a nearby table, grumbling under her breath as she picked up empty bottles and wiped the table clean. They smiled behind her back; Chrissie was entertaining when she got mad.

He settled into his usual spot at the end of the bar, resting against the cabinet with his arms crossed. What could have happened to make River take off like that? He'd wanted to watch her work with the customers with that determined look in her eyes. See her body move and imagine what it would feel like moving against him. His body instantly hardened—one spot in particular. His hunger for her morphed into frustration.

"So, you ready for your INSERV inspection next week?" Phillips asked after chugging his beer.

"As ready as I can be," he said, sizing up Phillips. "How was your leadership meeting this morning?"

Phillips chuckled. "It was fine, but if I have one more chief harassing me about singing 'Anchors Aweigh,' I think—"

"You think what? You're going to cry? Suck it up," said Shots, giving Phillips the look of death. "You have to earn your anchors. You'll learn the entire song. You'll run until we tell you to stop, and you'll do any and all the stupid things we ask of you."

"It's not like that," Phillips whispered. "I get messed up."

"You mean you get nervous," Bliss said. It wasn't so long ago, he was in Phillips's shoes. He'd only been a chief for the past six years and was up for senior chief. He could only get to master chief as an enlisted sailor. Going through transition to become a chief was one of the most important moments in a navy career. It was the only branch that changed the uniform of an E-7 and higher.

"I guess. I just . . . can't mess this up. I've been up for chief three times and only now made it. I want to do well in transition."

Logston slapped Phillips on the back. "You'll do great. You're a true Mayhem Manager."

Phillips glanced at Logston suspiciously. Bliss didn't blame him. Logston was seldom nice to anyone but himself.

He was a piece of work all right. But Bliss had his back. A redneck to the core, he busted his ass from sun up to sun down, as did all the Mayhem Managers. Logston took pride in his work and his craft.

"Why're you being nice?" Phillips asked.

"Oh, I don't know . . ." Logston looked up at the ceiling, rubbing a thumb over his scar. "Maybe because I'll be teaching leadership class tomorrow."

"Thanks for the warning. If I have to listen to you talk for an hour, I'll sneak in ear plugs."

The three men continued to harass each other, but Bliss could only think about River. Regardless of whatever set her off, she shouldn't have left. She had a shift to cover. Chrissie would have to close the place by herself. His frustration grew. Abruptly, he turned and marched to his office, leaving his friends to squabble among themselves.

He sank into the chair at his desk and pulled out the drawer that held his employee records. He thumbed through the files in alphabetical order. He didn't find River's. He flipped through them again. The vein in his forehead started to pulse and he slammed the drawer closed. Her file should be in there. *Rose.* She knew better than to put things out of order.

He fisted his hands and sat back in his chair, fuming. He heard his friends' laughter drift in from down the hall. Pushing to his feet, he walked over to the door and slammed it. He ached to laugh and be merry.

Chrissie said River had left in tears. He couldn't stand the thought. He slammed a fist against the door. Out of the corner of his eye, he caught sight of a vanilla folder set on the bookshelf. Hope bubbled up. He reached for it. *River Connelly* was written at the top of the file . . . her wrinkled application and paperwork. A smile tipped the corner of his mouth.

He carefully read her application, contemplating the address beneath her name. It struck a chord; it was familiar. He knew he'd seen it before. If he went to the address listed on her application, he would be violating every privacy law in California. He weighed it against his desire to see her.

Grinding his teeth as he considered his next move, he fisted the file in his hand opened it snapped a picture of the info with his phone, and shoved it into the file drawer. He was going to find out what was wrong. To ease the conflicted emotions twisting in his gut, he told himself, *I'm her boss. If something is going on that concerns my bar, I'm going to find out about it. Control and contain.*

He drove away with a mission, but with every light, every stop sign, a sinking feeling welded up inside him. Thanks to GPS, he pulled up to the address and parked his 1966 Ford Mustang. He got out, leaned on the hood of his car, and stared up at the second-floor windows of the house. He felt like a stalker.

Chicken. Either go up to the door or go back and help at WTF. He didn't know what River would think about him showing up like this. Hell, he didn't even know whether she was alone or had a boyfriend. With that thought, he pivoted around the car, stopped, cursed, and turned back around. He had to know if she was okay, and it wouldn't hurt to see if there were signs of a man around.

He strolled toward the porch. He beat his knuckles against the front door loudly and waited. He shook his head and rolled it around on his neck, trying to relax. The lock clicked and the door cracked open an inch.

He froze. He didn't know what to do. He always knew what to do. But stalker was uncharted territory for him. River had to know she was dealing with crazies when it came to everyone at WTF. The fight that occurred the first night he'd seen her, the interview with Rose freaking out on him, Sarah locking her in the bar, and now him standing on her porch. She had to have seen this coming.

"What're you doing here? How did you get my address?" she asked in a hoarse voice.

"Your employee paperwork." There was no point in lying to her.

"Why?" She opened the door wide and stepped onto the porch. Light from the living room streamed around her.

"I know I shouldn't have come. I wanted to make sure you were okay. Chrissie said you left in a hurry and were upset."

"Yes. I'm sorry. I had to leave. Something came up." Her gaze swept the floor and didn't come up to meet his.

Frustration, concern, and anxiety all converged at the exact same intersection, and he couldn't stand it. "River," he took a step closer. His gaze traveled over her face and searched her swollen eyes. He'd seen Rose's eyes like that many times over the past few months.

Tenderness filled him, and his heart hammered against his ribs. Before he had time to think, he lifted her chin, wanting to take away her sadness. She placed a hand on his chest but she didn't tell him to stop. He hesitated wrapping his arms around her waist. He gently pulled her into his embrace, needing to feel more of her.

He kissed her slowly and thoughtfully. He wanted her to enjoy his kiss and remember it. The touch of her lips was a delicious sensation. She tasted like lemon tea. He deepened the kiss, desire shooting through his body, finally untethered. He held her and skimmed his tongue over her lips, inviting her to join him. Hesitantly, her lips parted. His hunger grew. His kiss hardened, and she stiffened in his arms. Afraid he'd ruined the moment, he loosened his grip. To his delight, she wrapped her arms around his neck and matched his need with her own.

River was shocked and secretly thrilled by his advance. The feel of his lips on hers was her undoing. The heat of his body and the strength with which he held her proved without a doubt that Bliss was interested in her. Still, she found herself hesitating. Unwilling to let go and surrender to this man no matter how much she needed to. He was her boss, but for how long? She wasn't planning to stay in Oceanside. He knew that though; she'd told him in the interview, and he was still here despite it. It was such a small thing to cling to, but she did.

As he tightened his hold and his tongue caressed her lips, her restraint was chipped away. She closed her eyes. One taste wouldn't hurt anything. She parted her lips and allowed him to have a small piece of herself that she hadn't shared with any man for a long time.

She stood still for a moment. His muscles flexed, and the fear that he was going to pull away released something inside her. Desire not only for this moment, but for the possibility of a different life full of connection and friendship took hold. She wrapped her arms around his neck and deepened the kiss. Their tongues rolled together in an amazing dance of passion. She needed more. She ran her hand down his chest, over the tight muscles of his stomach, and skimmed her fingers under his shirt. Her body molded against him. She felt his heart thumping against her, as he groaned against her lips. What a sound that was . . . to hear him moan for her.

She nibbled his bottom lip and sucked on it for a moment. She felt his erection, hard and ready for her. Her core heated. She didn't know if she could give him more than this kiss. Being intimate had been a challenge since her assault.

He broke free of her kisses, touching her forehead to his, his breath caressing her.

"I should go," he whispered.

Her eyes flew open. Had he read her thoughts? "What . . . go?" Something inside her cried out for him to stay.

He stepped back, and she was staggered by the sudden loss of his hard body pressed against her. Her fingers touched her lips, missing his taste.

"If I don't go now, I won't be able to leave at all." He took a step back, then another, and then another,

She wanted to say something. She'd never experienced that kind of intensity before. He was worried about her, had come to check on her. And he took the chance to show he was interested in more than a working relationship. Somehow, she knew Bliss didn't do this kind of thing and her heart softened for him. Before he reached his car, she glimpsed a smile on his sexy lips. She was intrigued by the mystery that was Maddox Bliss.

CHAPTER FIFTEEN

River was on autopilot—numb, cold—and she had withdrawn deep into herself. She made it through the meeting with Mathew's life insurance agent and with the real-estate agent about putting his house on the market. She wanted the day to be over, but she still had to get through a night shift at WTF.

She hesitated, then steeled herself and plowed through the door, only to be met with resistance. A screech came from the other side, and she cautiously peeked in and around the door. A tall curvy blonde was hopping up and down on a booted foot, boobs busting out of a halter-top. She had a broom in her hand. River then realized the resistance had been Sarah.

"Fuck! Shit! Balls! Damn it all to hell," Sarah shouted, her face crunched up in pain.

River stepped back and closed the door. *Great.* She pushed the door slowly this time and strolled in as if nothing happened. She knew Sarah liked theatrics, so if she just ignored her, Sarah would have no stage for her drama.

Sarah was sitting in a chair rubbing her big toe. She shot River a dark look. "You're late. I'm going to dock your pay fifteen minutes," she snapped.

River walked to the storage room. "Be my guest," she

replied, not bothering to look back. She had more on her mind than a lousy two dollars, and at this point, it was worth it to see Sarah hopping around like that. It almost made up for Sarah locking her in the bar that first night they worked together.

She set her purse down on an empty shelf in the storage room, then grabbed the clipboard that was hanging next to the door and scanned the order list. She strolled over to the first shelf, counted bottles of alcohol, and wrote down what they needed. A few minutes passed, and then she noticed Sarah glaring at her from the door.

"You better think twice about running out on me like you did to Chrissie last night."

She cringed. How did Sarah know about that already? An image of Bliss and Rose surfaced and she shook it off. She couldn't let Sarah see her upset. She withdrew deep into herself where no one could find her.

"It won't happen again," she said in a monotone voice, continuing to count bottles.

The sound of her voice was hauntingly familiar. Empty. No hope, no joy, no sadness, no pain, only emptiness. Sarah stepped back into the hall, flipping her hair as she left. River exhaled, closing her eyes. *Eight hours to go.*

For the next few hours, River did anything and everything she could to stay out of Sarah's way, but for a Wednesday night the bar was packed. River tried not to worry.

"What can I get you?" she asked a young man who was drooling over Sarah. She tapped her knuckles against the countertop to get his attention.

"Her," he moaned.

"Trust me, you don't want her," she replied.

"Shot of Patrón and a Coors."

"Coming up." She was starting to remember where things were, and her turnover rate was much higher now. A moment later, she handed him a shot and a beer. "Seven bucks."

He tossed eight bucks onto the counter and wandered off.

"I'll take a Red Bull," Logston said in deep voice as he approached. He muscled in between two men at the bar and stationed himself in front of her. "Hi, sweet cheeks, did you miss me? I missed you."

She wanted to roll her eyes. "Sure thing." She deliberately ignored his question as she got his drink from the mini-fridge down below. "Three bucks." She placed the drink in front of him.

"Start a tab for me."

"Okay." She swung around and stared at the register. She didn't know how to do that. Now she really rolled her eyes. "Sarah, how do I start a tab?"

"Seriously? What did Chrissie teach you?" Sarah complained, stomping toward her. She pushed River aside. "Watch. You touch here, open a bill, and then touch this. Just keep adding drinks." She walked back to her end of the bar. "Oh, and keep an eye on him." Sarah shot a death glare at Logston. "He drinks too much. He will be drunk in no time if you don't mother him. And Bliss doesn't tolerate anyone getting drunk in his bar, friend or not." Sarah swept around to help a customer, then stopped and said, "Go clean up the tables."

For starters, she hadn't seen everything Sarah had done on the screen, and she sure as hell didn't want to go out into the crowd and clean tables. She was running on empty and just wanted to go home and curl into a ball and cry.

Logston popped the top of his drink. It drew River's attention. He chugged his Red Bull and gave out a loud belch. She decided she'd take the crowd over Logston staring at her. He was just a flirt, but it got old.

She snatched a tray off a shelf and plowed into the crowd as fast as she could. She didn't look at anyone, only moved from table to table gathering glasses and empty beer bottles. She cleared three tables before she hurried back to the bar.

"Wow, dang sugar, that was fast. Did it hurt to be away from me for so long?" asked Logston, thumbing the scar on his jaw.

She managed a wan smile, grabbed another tray, and once again pushed into the crowd. This time she headed for the patio where there were fewer people.

Outside, she dropped the tray onto a nearby table and sank into a chair. The dark evening sky blanketed her. Her lower eyelid twitched. She dropped her face into her hands miserably. Things had been going surprisingly well—working at WTF, living in Oceanside—but after today she was falling apart. She could almost feel Mathew's disappointment from the other side. Her guts twisted into knots. Her entire body started to shake.

"You all right?" came Chrissie's perky voice. River lifted her head. Her favorite bartender was sitting two tables across from her.

"I'm fine. What are you doing here? Isn't it your night off?"

"Sarah isn't the only one who comes here to drink on her night off. Guilty as charged!" Chrissie raised her hand, which clutched a cigarette, high into the air.

River sat back, her poor mood eased a little.

Chrissie took a long drag off her cigarette, sucking in her cheeks. She wore short-shorts. Her legs stretched out in front of her, as if she didn't have a care in the world. River couldn't remember the last time she was able to relax like that.

"Why do you guys do that?"

Chrissie raised a brow. "Do what?"

"Come here on your nights off. I mean, don't you get tired of being here?"

"Never. This place is my home, and these people are my

family. Family I want to kill sometimes, but family all the same."

River laughed, and then a wide smile spread across her face.

"So, what's your story?" Chrissie took another drag off her cigarette and exhaled a cloud of smoke. She held the cigarette out to River. "Want a drag? Looks like you need it more than I do."

"No thanks. I don't smoke. Tried once and threw up."

Chrissie burst into laughter.

River leaned to the side of the chair and tucked her feet next to her butt, but then she caught herself and sat up quickly. That was something she only did when she talked to Mathew. It felt odd, but not terrible, to be comfortable enough to do it in front of Chrissie.

"I'm waiting," Chrissie said.

River was tugged back to the present. "My story, right? What do you want to know?"

"For starters, what brought you here? I mean, to work at WTF?"

She studied Chrissie for a long while. She didn't know why, but it was easy being around her. Was she ready to talk about Mathew? Was she ready to start letting go? She didn't know, but she was willing to try. She swallowed, took a breath, and forced the words to form on her tongue.

"My brother died a few weeks ago. I had to come to town and take care of his estate."

Chrissie's eyes rounded. "I'm sorry to hear that. Your brother. That stinks." The surprise in her voice didn't match her sad expression.

"Yes, it does." Hot tears threatened to fall.

"How did he die, if you don't mind me asking?"

"A car accident. He was hit head-on by a drunk driver a block or so away."

Chrissie sat up, looking a little pale. "So that brought you here?"

River got the feeling the friendly conversation had turned sour. "Yes and no. He came here—"

"What the hell is this, social hour?" Sarah shouted from the doorway. She shot River an I-hate-you glare and then stared at Chrissie.

Chrissie put on her grumpy face, as River liked to call it. It was a face Chrissie reserved for Sarah alone. "Why yes it is," she said to Sarah.

"It is busy. Why don't you come in and put in some extra hours?" Sarah said dryly.

Chrissie didn't reply.

Sarah let out an exasperated sigh and turned her attention back to River. "Come on. I need help behind the bar."

Next thing she knew, Sarah had clamped her fingers around her arm and painfully hauled her to her feet. Her claws dug into her flesh as she was pulled toward the bar. She yanked free and rooted herself to the floor.

"What're you doing? Don't touch me."

"Socializing is not in your job description. I know because I helped draft it," Sarah snapped. She crossed her arms under her breasts, hoisting them up higher for everyone to see.

"I was taking my fifteen-minute break. I do get one of those, don't I?" River said, trying to bottle her anger.

"Yes, you do. Between your second and third hour of work, if you're working an eight-hour shift. But here's the catch: I have to authorize it and I didn't. Now, get back to work."

River was really starting to hate Sarah with a passion. *Why is she such a bitch?* She didn't argue anymore, but she did slam her shoulder against Sarah's, shoving her as she went past. She could be a bitch too.

By the time she had returned from the patio, Logston was

dancing with two women on the dance floor. She'd been happy to see him occupied. The night went by in a blur after that. She mixed and served drink after drink until she lost count.

After her shift, she dashed out of the bar before Sarah could lock her in again. She felt confident that she did a good job in spite of the small incident with Sarah. It seemed repetition was the key to bartending. *Progress.*

As she reached her car, she unscrewed her fake smile and a heavy iciness settled on her. Another night in Mathew's quiet house. She shuddered. The crashing waves played a melody out on the wind. Her eyes drifted to the dark windows of the loft. Disappointment washed over her and took her by surprise. It would have been nice to see Bliss. He would have been a welcome distraction tonight.

Sighing, she climbed into her car then waited for Sarah to exit WTF. She might not care for Sarah, but there was no way she was going to let her walk out into a dark parking lot alone. The way men buzzed around her, surely she had concerns about the possibility one of them might be lurking in the shadows.

River picked at her black fitted pants. *Did Sarah and Bliss have more than just a working relationship? Were they a couple at one point? Is that why he kept her around?*

Ugh . . . how was she supposed to compete against Sarah? No. She wasn't traveling the path of doubt. Bliss wouldn't have kissed her if Sarah was in the picture.

She closed her eyes and ran a finger over her lips. She could still taste his sweetness. Her breath hitched in her throat as her pulse quickened with desire. Lost in the moment, she could feel how tightly he held her. It was delicious to feel so alive even if for a second. She fanned herself and opened her eyes. She was fogging up her mirror. She peered around the parking lot. Sarah's car was gone. She must have missed her leaving while she was daydreaming.

Just then, one of the lights in the loft turned on. He passed in front of a window wearing the green flight suit she'd seen some of the men wear at the unit when she visited. He tossed something down and unzipped the flight suit. The temptation to watch was unbearable, but she didn't want to get caught peeping. She started the car, eyes still glued to the window. Her headlights automatically turned on, and Bliss looked down at her from the window.

"Oh crap." Heat flooded her cheeks as she fumbled to get her seatbelt on. She quickly put the gear in reverse, backed the car, turned to face to road . . . and screamed. He was standing in her way. She planned to drive around him, but when he realized her intention, he slapped his hands down on the hood. Her pulse hammered as he bent over her hood . . . in a white undershirt and boxers. *What is it with him being half-naked all the time? And how the hell did he get down here so fast?* She put the car in park and breathed deeply. *Just say you were leaving.*

"What are you doing? Trying to give me a heart attack?" she asked, rolling down her window.

He raised a brow and sauntered over to her. She hated it when he did that. It made her feel like she was in trouble.

"Come have a drink with me." He rested an arm on the top of the car and gazed down at her with his all-consuming golden eyes.

"It's almost three-thirty. I need to go home."

Bliss brushed her neck with his fingers. "Please."

His tone was tender and sweet. If she'd been standing, her knees would have buckled. It was a tone she would never have thought possible from this tough man.

"I . . . really should go. It has been a long day," she stammered.

He opened the door and held out a hand. She let out a defeated sigh, rolled up the window, and turned off the engine. She took his hand, not knowing what to expect or what she was getting herself into, but she didn't have the energy to care.

He rubbed the pad of his thumb over her fingers and her core tightened. Pulling her closer, he closed the door behind her, backing her up against it. He lowered his head and took a deep breath, inhaling the scent of her hair and neck. It seemed barbaric, yet it excited her immensely.

"I've been thinking about you all day, and the thought of not seeing you before you left had me chewing out my crew all night." He pressed his hips gently against hers, showing his need.

She couldn't deny she'd been waiting for him. She'd wanted to see him, and that frightened her. Was she ready to let someone else in her life?

"Bliss . . ."

"Come on." He pushed away from the car with her hand anchored to his and led her back to WTF.

CHAPTER SIXTEEN

B liss wasn't letting her get away. She was having a drink with him, like it or not. Truth be told, she liked that he made the decision for her. He was practically dragging her up the stairs two at a time. She didn't want to think about how deep into uncharted waters she was getting. *Just go with it,* she told herself.

He pushed the door open and stepped aside for River to enter. As she passed, she tried to avert her eyes from his boxer shorts. He walked to a small dresser next to his bed and pulled out a pair of boxers and loose black athletic pants.

"Water's in the fridge. I'm going to take a quick shower. I smell like the craft." He turned and locked eyes with her. There was softness in them. "Don't leave . . . please. I'll only be a minute."

She didn't say a word, only nodded.

"Have a look around." He strode to his bathroom door, gave River a hungry glance, and then slipped inside.

River wasn't so sure about being up here with Bliss alone. She walked over to the small kitchen area and ran a hand over the cold white counter. A kitchen said a lot about a person, and this kitchen reminded her of a hospital. She opened a nearby cupboard; there were four white ceramic plates on one shelf, four glasses on another, and four white ceramic bowls on a third shelf. *Four must be his number.* Next, she went to the other side of the stove and opened another cupboard, only to find a few spices. She wondered how he could live with so little. But the more she thought about it, the more appealing it became. He wasn't tied to "things," unlike most people. He wasn't like most people . . . not that she'd ever believed he was. She might have more in common with this proud and overly confident man than she first thought. If Bliss's father owned this building, she wondered if this was where Bliss and Rose had grown up.

She wandered over to a window and watched the moonlight glimmer off the ocean as the waves rolled in. Spying a latch at the edge of the window, River pushed the base out and the window tilted open. The night air tumbled all around her. She wrapped her arms around herself and breathed the salty air. She closed her eyes, listening to the sound of the waves. She was becoming accustomed to their rhythmic cadence.

The sound of a cupboard banging close almost made her jump out of her skin.

"Water?" Bliss asked in a deep voice.

He stood at the island with a bottle of water and a glass.

She managed a, "Yes, please." His magnificent bare chest was still damp with droplets from his shower. Her body responded with a wave of heat. She inwardly groaned and walked toward him.

He handed her the glass, and then he leaned back against the counter studying her. His pants rode low on his hips. She could see the tapering of muscles down into forbidden terrain. She looked away and tried not to let him see how she wanted him. He was way too good looking.

"So, how was work?" he asked.

"Fine," she spat out. "Logston said you had a night mission."

"Yeah, had to get in my night hours."

"Hours?" she asked, wrinkling her nose at him.

His smile made her toes curl. Placing his hands on the counter, he lifted his weight slightly. Every ab muscle flexed and his chest popped out. Instantly, she forgot what they were talking about. She struggled to focus. *Get a grip! Yeah, I'd sure like a grip of those . . .*

"Every craftmaster is required to have a certain number of day and night hours to maintain his qualification to drive. Nothing really exciting, driving around, running drills, and showboating a little."

"Showboating. What's that?"

He smiled. "Showboating is what we call 'showing off'. Not everyone has skills like I do, so I have to give the other guys a role model."

And arrogant is back. River laughed and rolled her eyes, feeling some of her anxiety lifting from the day. He pulled out a barstool tucked under the counter. River accepted and took a seat. Then he tugged open the fridge and peered inside.

It was packed with food, nothing at all like the cupboards. There were strawberries, apples, kiwis, grapes, salad, orange and red peppers, and much more. He was a health-conscious man, and here she'd thought all he did was work out and drink beer. Irritation bubbled in her chest, not with Bliss, but with herself. She'd made so many judgments about him.

"What should we have? I'm starving." He grabbed a few things and tossed them onto the counter. "Fruit salad." He retrieved a knife and a cutting board and began dicing an apple.

"You don't have to feed me. I really should be getting home." She started to stand up, but he pointed his knife at her.

"Sit down. We're spending time together." He went back to dicing.

She didn't know how to respond to that, so she sat back down as commanded. He displayed a pleased smirk at her blind obedience. She frowned. If that had been Mathew, she would have stuck out her tongue. She found she couldn't do that with Bliss. She did want to spend time with him—get to know him.

"So, was it busy downstairs today?" he asked.

"It wasn't too bad. One good thing about being busy is that time goes by so fast," she said, stealing three green grapes off the bunch sitting in front of her. She rolled them around in her fingers, seeing if they were firm. Then she popped one in her mouth and crushed it between her teeth. The juice coated her tongue. She tried to remember if she'd eaten anything today. She didn't recall thinking about food at all. Her stomach rumbled so loudly Bliss glanced over at her.

"And you were going to leave." He pulled off a few more grapes and held one up to her mouth. He wore an easy smile, but his eyes told another story altogether. They were more brown than amber now. Was this small act of wanting to feed her an invitation to something more? *Breathe* . . .

He didn't say a word. He held perfectly still and waited for her to make the next move. She went against every carefully constructed wall she'd built up around herself. Right now, she was all in. She was ready to focus on this moment. She slowly leaned toward his outstretched hand. She didn't take her eyes off him. She wanted to remember this moment of self-indulgence. She wanted to be the woman she remembered she could be.

The light in his eyes brightened as she took the grape into her mouth, allowing her lips to skim over his fingers. His jaw clenched and . . . was that a moan?

"Shit!" Bliss said, cheeks coloring slightly.

She didn't know why, but she laughed while trying not to choke on the grape. She liked seeing him squirm.

She held a grape out to him, arching her brow in challenge. He didn't skip a beat. He strolled around the island. She held the grape up to his mouth and he lowered his head. Gently, he took the grape between his teeth and squished it. The juice squirted out, and she laughed again as a handsome smile spread across his face. He chuckled and placed his hands on her thighs as if it was the most natural thing in the world. He gazed at her with such hunger she wanted nothing more than to wrap her arms around his neck. He brushed his lips over hers.

She sucked in a breath. "I was disappointed when Logston said you weren't coming to the bar."

"Disappointed . . ." He ran his fingers through her hair. "Well, Miss Connelly, I can't have that." He captured her lips in a hungry kiss, sending spirals of ecstasy throughout her body.

Oh dear God, she tasted like desire. Bliss ran his fingers through River's long, silky hair and along the base of her skull. *Careful with her. You must stay in control.* He released her lips hesitantly and she moaned. He explored her ivory skin, showering it with feather-soft kisses. Around her lips and along her jaw, he traveled down her neck. Pausing at the base of her throat where her pulse hammered. The growing heat River caused within him stocked hot as embers. Soon he would be burned alive. His hands traveled over the planes of her back and rested on her round hips, gripping them firmly. He wanted this woman badly; every cell in his body ached for her. Her lips, her touch, her desire. She moaned as he caressed the tops of her breasts. His body shook with need and he held back. Wanting her to want him, wanting her to need him. He placed one soft kiss on the top of her heaving chest, then crashed his lips to hers.

He pulled her up with one hand from the barstool, securing her tightly against his burning body, while the other hand moved to the top buttons of her blouse. She froze when he unfastened them. Bliss pulled back and frowned. He searched her eyes, needing to know if he had gone too far. She glided her fingers over the muscles of his back, emitting a sigh as she stroked his skin, his self-control was slipping with every touch she bestowed on him. His doubt beginning to fade.

"I should go," she breathed, dark lashes fluttering.

No. Please, no.

"Why? I thought you were enjoying yourself." He undid a third button just under her breasts and pushed the fabric aside. A black lace bra cradled well-shaped breasts. He admired them for a moment. *Dear God, she's perfect.* Unable to resist, he cupped her breast. Again, she moaned . . . and the heavenly sound was almost his undoing.

"You're my boss."

"If it's a problem, I'll fire you." He kissed her gently, wanting to persuade her to stay with him.

She shoved his chest playfully and gave him a breathtaking smile. Her smile reminded him of someone. There was something in that smile . . . if only he could place it.

"I have to go. I'll see you later." She stepped away from him, allowing her fingers to run over his muscles.

He reached out, wanting to stay connected to her as long as he could. She was right. He was her boss. It wasn't professional of him to lust after his newest bartender. A bartender, he reminded himself, who was only temporary. He wanted to shred that word to pieces.

"Thank you for the grapes." She strolled over to the door. He didn't follow. He knew if he did she would never be allowed to leave. He didn't know if he was ready for that.

❦

He's my boss. I'm here to pack up Mathew's house and sell it, not to get involved with anyone. These thoughts raced through her head as River quickly left Bliss's grasp and bee-lined for the door.

She grabbed the doorknob and flung the door open, and then a rough hand swiftly pulled her back. She gasped. He was there behind her. One of his powerful arms wrapped around her waist, and it was too tight. Painful.

Suddenly she was next to the river, captured. She bucked against his body and yanked away. She broke free and ran. It wasn't until she at her car that she was able to process where she was and what she was doing. Her body shook violently. She braced herself against the car. *Deep breath in, deep breath out.* She started to sob. She just wanted things to be like before her attack. Have a normal moment with a guy she thought was sexy and kind. But she couldn't. She screamed into the night air. That man who attacked her had taken so much from her. She didn't trust people easily. She stayed home to avoid running the risk of something happening like that again, and all the stupid triggers.

Soft footsteps came up behind her. She spun around and Bliss held up his hands.

"Are you okay? I didn't mean to scare you." Every line in Bliss's face seem a mile deep.

She wiped her tears away, feeling mortified. Her entire body flushed under the look of concern on his face. "I . . . I'm sorry," she said, pulling out her keys. "I really have to go."

He placed a hand on the car door so she couldn't open it. She didn't want to talk about what just happened. "Bliss, please . . . let me go."

"No. Not until you tell me what just happened. You're not leaving here scared of anything I did . . ." He looked away.

"Why does it matter?"

"It matters to me. I've watched my sister for weeks get jumpy like that and I have a feeling why. I couldn't live with myself if I was the cause for that kind of reaction."

"Bliss, it wasn't anything you did . . . well, you did . . . but . . . shit, you didn't." She ran a hand through her hair. She felt trapped. Her heart broke a little from the hurt in his tone. She didn't want him to know about what happened to her. She did want him thinking he was the cause for the reaction either though.

The words spilled out. "When I was in college, I was attacked. He grabbed me from behind." Her throat locked up. She didn't want the memory to surface again. It was to crippling. "The way you grabbed me . . . it triggered my panic. It's not your fault, you didn't know. I can control it most of the time, but lately I have been pushing my luck being around so many people. If my anxiety gets too high, it doesn't take much to set the memory off."

Bliss blew out a breath she hadn't see him hanging on to. His body relaxed for a moment, but the look on his face was sad. She moved his hand from the car, wanting to be done with this conversation. She couldn't have him looking all sad for her. That was why she never told Mathew, because of that very look. No. She wasn't going to be the victim.

"I'm sorry," he said in a whisper.

"I am too." She climbed in the car, but before she closed the door, she said, "I knocked him out and I got away before . . . before he could . . ." Next the door slammed, and she headed for Mathew's. She gave herself over to the numb, empty feeling clinging to her skin. The perfect end to a perfectly shitty day.

CHAPTER SEVENTEEN

River placed a stack of empty boxes on the floor next to Mathew's closet and ran her hand over his clothes. Having looked through every drawer, every cabinet, shelf, and closet corner in the entire house, she thought starting with Mathew's clothes would be the easiest to go through and pack what she wanted and donate the rest. She clenched her teeth together and clutched a handful of hangers. She yanked the shirts free and set them on the floor. One at a time she looked at the shirts, and images of Mathew formed in her mind of him wearing them. She picked a few that she liked and knew she would wear and thrust them into a box closest to her. Then scooped up the others and placed them into the donation box. *They're just things . . .* She stared at what once belonged to her brother and grief struck her hard and fast. *His things . . .* Loneliness tumbled through her, worse than if she were an awkward teen abandoned at the prom.

Her best friend was gone. She thought of Bliss and how good he made her feel. How when he smiled at her, her heart responded from the deepest part of her. But it didn't work. Her happy thoughts skedaddled away. She was once again in a gray world.

She pushed the box against the wall. What was she going to do with all of Mathew's stuff? She'd already been in town for three weeks. She had three weeks left of vacation and another week of sick leave. If she got her shit together, she might not need more time than that. She peered around the room trying not to feel overwhelmed. All of his stuff wasn't going to fit in her small house. She would have to rent a storage POD. That way, she could store it in her driveway back home until she found the strength to get rid of some of it.

She made it through the closet and took the donation boxes downstairs and out into the garage. Anxiety was spreading its crippling fingers around her chest. A shower would help.

She rummaged through her clothes for something to change in to and then sauntered into Mathew's bathroom. Thoughts of Bliss surfaced again. It was time she examined how he made her feel and whether it was a good thing. After last night she wasn't so sure. Even if by some miracle she stayed in town longer, could she really work through her issues and have a relationship with him?

It had not been her intention to be attracted to her boss—a cocky, stubborn but considerate, caring, and handsome man. She sighed dreamily, then sobered. *I sure as hell had no intention of getting into any sort of relationship. But isn't that what I'm doing? Starting a relationship with Bliss? It's fair to say we don't have a strictly platonic relationship anymore. What do I want that to mean?*

She set her clothes down by the sink, turned on the shower, and began to undress. Her last boyfriend was when she was a freshman in college, and that only lasted a semester. She was a bit rusty, but she figured it was safe to say they were dating. She wrinkled her nose. That wasn't quite accurate. This was Bliss after all. She liked him, but didn't that mean she cared about him? How could she have a relationship with a man she expected to leave? *Do I want to stay and see if things could become more? Will I finally be able to move past my assault?*

As she drove into the parking lot, not a single parking spot was open. *This can't be good.* She circled the parking lot twice before giving up and parking in the lot across the street at a dry cleaner.

As she headed toward WTF, she heard music in the distance. When she pulled open the door, her eardrums were blasted by the loud sound. She halted on the other side, rising on tiptoes to see the stage. She could only see blonde hair.

She searched for the best path to the bar, and then she squeezed in and around people who were talking and dancing, making her path torturous. It reminded her of the first night she'd come to WTF to scope out the place. Tentatively, she made her way forward. People brushed her arms and her sides. She kept working her way toward the bar. On approach, she spied Sarah and Chrissie buzzing around, mixing and serving drinks.

She was two people deep from breaking free of the crowd when a large hand clasped her wrist and started to pull her back. She couldn't see who had a hold on her. Twisting her arm, she tried to break free, but the iron grip didn't budge. She bit the inside of her cheek, stopping herself from crying out. *I will not cower . . .*

She continued to resist, bumping this person and that person, as she was pulled, not so gently, through the crowd. Not two minutes ago, she had danced around them all, not wanting to make contact. Now she was shoving, squeezing, and groping at people as she got dragged off to who knew where. Still, she didn't make a sound to gripped by fear.

Inwardly groaning in frustration, she pulled at the fingers crushing her wrist. Just as she managed to get close enough to the hand to sink her teeth into it, she found herself on the dance floor. Logston smiled mischievously at her as he twirled her around.

Logston. Fury boiled. The nerve of him, scaring the crap out of her. Her fury mixed with a small rush of relief that, at least, it was someone she knew. She loosened up and allowed Logston to dance around like a madman.

"You know, you could have just asked me if I wanted to dance instead of dragging me out here like some barbarian!" she shouted.

Logston smiled. "I dragged you out here because you would have told me no."

"That's not true," she said, punching his wide chest a little too aggressively. Her anger subsiding . . . a little after she punched him once more.

He spun her out and then pulled her back in, keeping her tight against his body. "All the women tell me no. That's why I didn't ask."

"No."

"Yes," he said with a faint smile that held a touch of sadness.

There was something in his tone that pulled at her heartstrings. This was the first true and honest moment they shared. A wave of compassion washed over her, and she began to dance with feeling. Glancing at the stage, she saw Phillips singing his heart out. As her eyes swept the crowd and noted all the bright and happy faces, she realized why the parking lot was packed. They were here to listen to Phillips. *Wow.*

Logston twirled her and sent her shooting out. She laughed as he pulled her back against his chest.

"You're going to make me late for work, and then Sarah will be in a bad mood for the rest of the night."

"She's always in a bad mood," he replied, doing the two-step and swinging her around again.

She had to admit for a big guy he sure could dance. She let him enjoy himself for a minute more, and then she gave him a death stare. "You're going to get me in trouble. I'll find you on my fifteen-minute break and we can dance again."

He winked. "Fine." Logston gave her a final spin and released her hand.

Caught off guard, she found herself bouncing into the chest of a young, smiling stranger.

"Sorry."

"No worries. Run into me anytime," said the young man with a wink.

She edged past him and worked her way to the bar again, emerging successfully this time.

From behind the bar, she paused to survey her surroundings. A group of guys in the corner laughed at one another for their lack of pool skills while their female counterparts were giggling as they watched Phillips sing.

The patio doors were open wide and the salty air sailed around. It was a beautiful evening. The shadows of dusk eased their way into the Whiskey-Tango-Foxtrot. The place seemed. . . happy. She realized that WTF was always happy. Everyone was of a teasing nature and polite. Come to think of it, Sarah was the only one who seemed to mess with the cheerful energy this place gave off. There was something about Sarah that made River's temper crouch, ready to spring and attack.

River could see what attracted her brother to this place— it was an escape. WTF was the go-to place when you wanted to forget your troubles. If she hadn't been such a spaz, she would have seen that right away. This was Mathew's haven.

The room changed for her. Instead of seeing strangers, she saw Mathew's friends. Men he'd have shared a drink with and swapped stories with. Women he could have asked to dance with or perhaps shared a night with. She felt Mathew all around her, and suddenly, she wasn't so alone.

Unshed tears blurred her vision. She wasn't going to cry, not at work. Dashing down the hall before anyone could notice, she retrieved her cash drawer for the night. A minute later, she returned behind the bar and Chrissie bounced over to her.

"Doesn't he sound great?"

River was confused for a second, then she realized Chrissie was talking about Phillips. "Yes. He's very good."

"I know, right?" Chrissie stared dreamy-eyed at Phillips, obviously crushing on him. She removed her cash drawer, and not taking her eyes off Phillips, she wandered down the hall, swaying and singing along with his music. River chuckled at her new friend. Yes, Chrissie was her friend.

Bracing herself for the work ahead, she got her game face on by gluing on her smile. She parted a chunk of her bangs and swept them across her forehead. Tending the bar was getting easier. The movement of it was a kind of dance she enjoyed, like reading one of her manuscripts. She frowned. She did miss her stories.

Before serving her customers, she scanned the open tabs. There were three. One was Logston's, and the other two she didn't know anything about. She walked back to the office where Chrissie was counting out her till. She popped her head in.

"Who has the two tabs running?"

Chrissie didn't look up at her but said, "The five guys in the back corner by the pool tables watching Phillips, and the other is the older guy at the bar with the gray-and-black beard."

"Okay, thanks."

Chrissie flashed her a serious look. "Keep an eye on the one with the beard. He's had three drinks and it's only been an hour."

River knew the four-drinks, two-hour rule, and went back out to the bar. The live music had stopped and happy chatter filled the air. Phillips was seated two barstools away from the man with the peppered beard. She studied the man for a second. He was facing Phillips, and they were having an exchange about TCU. *Ugh, football.*

She turned back toward the crowd. Everyone was in good spirits, and most had drinks in their hands as they milled about. She was wrong to think it'd be a stressful night for her.

Phillips was the star of the night. His emerald green eyes sparkled at her, and then he tipped his chin. She walked over, getting used to the "come over here" gesture. "What can I get you?" she said.

"Budweiser. Please." Phillips plunked some change and a few dollars on the counter.

"Are you done with your set?" she asked.

"No, taking a break. I'll sing again around six. I was only teasing the crowd."

She grabbed his beer out of the fridge and popped the top with a cap opener in front of him. Her gaze slid over his sharp features, admiring his smooth skin. With his tan and blond hair, he looked like the beach Ken doll she'd played with as a girl.

"So, where are Shots and Bliss?"

Phillips's perfect lips pressed to his bottle and he drank a mouthful. He looked good even just doing that simple act. She sighed out loud, thinking of Bliss. She was anxious to see how he would interact with her after yesterday.

Phillips's bottle tapped the lacquered counter. "Bliss and Shots are busy working out and going for a run. Bunch of health nuts those two. They're planning to cover ten miles." He motioned for her to get closer and she leaned in. He held up a hand and shielded his mouth as if to tell her a secret. "Get this . . . just because they want to. What a pair of wackos." He laughed, amused with himself. She found his laughter infectious, and she chuckled along with him.

"What's wrong with a good long run? I—"

"Get me another drink," the man with the peppered beard said.

River blinked at the interruption. "What're you having?" she asked, feeling all the enthusiasm Phillips had just invoked leak out of her feet.

"Vodka straight, with ice." The man pushed his glass over to her.

She pulled her hair over her shoulder and stood there a minute. Should she tell him this was his last drink or wait to see if he would ask for another one? Not wanting a confrontation, she chose to wait it out. She took the glass and then placed it with the other used glasses. She went to retrieve a clean one. She poured the man's drink and placed it in front of him.

Phillips gave her a strange look. She didn't know why, but she was sure she had lost her smile and was now sour-faced. She stepped back and struggled to plaster the fake smile back in place.

"Don't hurt yourself," said Phillips, giving her a half-smile before taking another swallow of beer.

"I won't, if only I can get this smile to stay in place."

"Talk about tortured. What's the problem?"

She thought of asking Phillips about the rule but decided against it. Not sure she really wanted to know.

"Nothing."

"Right, and I'm fat and ugly," he said, narrowing his eyes. He peered over his shoulder at Sarah as her voice rose over the chatter in the bar.

What's with all these guys thinking they're God's gift to women? Yes, they were good looking, but did they have to like it so much? She stared off at the other end of the bar. Sarah's wrist was being held tightly by a young man, forcing her closer to him. Just as Phillips began to rise out of his seat, Sarah reached for a glass of water and splashed it in the young man's face. The young man released her wrist.

"You're cut off, Bricker. You know the rules. Drink some water and I'll think about letting you have another drink,"

Sarah said cuttingly.

"Come on, Sarah. Water?" complained the young man, wiping his face on his shirt.

Phillips sat back down and ran a hand through his hair, looking grim. "This four-drink rule is killing the guys."

She eyed him. "So, this is a new rule?" she asked.

"Yes, Bliss has been enforcing it hardcore for the past few weeks."

"Why?" she asked.

"Bad shit happened, and he feels like it's his fault." Phillips shrugged. "I mean I get it. He feels responsible . . ."

The bar erupted into chaos. Cries and hollering rang out everywhere. Phillips swung around to see what the commotion was about. Some of the men in the bar gave each other high-fives and chest bumps. Others waved their friends off and grumbled under their breath.

"Can you believe that? People still arm wrestle?" the bearded man said, standing up. He tossed a twenty and a ten on the counter and walked into the crowd. River watched him leave and breathed a sigh of relief. She didn't have to confront him about the rule. She picked up the cash and closed out his bill.

After the bearded man left, she tried to relax, but a wave of orders hit. Feeling her stomach knot, she said a little prayer and continued taking orders.

It was an hour later before she had a chance to catch her breath. Phillips was getting ready to sing again, and all the women herded around the small stage. The pool tables were all full, and others waited their turn. She handed a sweet-looking young man two beers. He handed her cash and walked away from the bar. Pushing a strand of hair behind her ear, she decided she needed a pee break.

"Sarah, I'll be right back," she shouted toward the other end of the bar. Sarah jerked around and glared.

And then she caught a glimpse of the bearded man. She thought he'd left. The young man she'd just served handed his two beers to the man with the beard. *Shit.* She wrinkled her nose. Anger coursed through her veins at the thought of those men breaking the rules. It did seem an odd rule to have. A slow thought surfaced. Could the rule have to do with Mathew's Death? Crossing her legs, she did a little dance. She would have to check on him later. Nature called.

It had been an hour since she'd last served the bearded man, so maybe she was in the clear. She studied him a little more closely as he took one of the beers. He tipped it up toward the young man. Beer sloshed all over the tabletop and he laughed hysterically, quite amused.

Not good. She did a little dance again and headed for the bathroom.

CHAPTER EIGHTEEN

Shots gripped the car door as he got out and stood on his sore, aching legs. "I just had a conversation with my calves, and they said they hate you."

Bliss smirked. He had a crusty layer of salt coating his body from the intense workout he'd put himself and Shots through. He was desperate to work off this pent-up energy he'd been dealing with ever since River ran out on him. The thought of someone trying to hurt her made his guts turn. Her words kept playing over and over in his mind, "I got away before . . .", then an image of Rose's bruised wrists flashed in his head and the urge to kill Chapman amplified.

"Tell your calves to quit bitching," he replied. Shots hobbled down the side alley toward the stairs to the loft. Bliss almost felt sorry for him . . . *almost*. PRTs were only a few weeks away, and Shots needed to do a little more running. Not to mention, they would be running with the guys going through Transition.

Shots flipped him the bird. "I'm taking an hour-long shower. Water bill's on you."

Bliss burst out in laughter at his friend, surprising himself. It felt good to have a bit of happiness override his tightly bound emotions. He pulled out his phone and checked to see if he had any calls from Rose. The baby was due any day and he was getting nervous.

Rose leaving, the baby coming, and River waltzing into his life was a bit more than his emotional management skills could handle. All it took was a snarky tone from a friend and he was ready for a verbal sparring match. No missed calls. He shoved his phone back into his running shorts.

An unusual movement caught his eye just past a blue Ford Ranger. A man was swaying on his feet, trying to work his key into the lock of the vehicle door. It was obvious the man was drunk. Black, icy fear laced around his chest, making it hard to breathe. If he had arrived two minutes earlier to WTF, he would have missed stopping this man. He closed his eyes and sent a silent prayer to God. When he opened his eyes, the helpless fear of another drunk managing to slip past his vigil and killing someone twisted and turned in his gut. Wagner's tombstone stool his mind. Then it distorted into a burning hatred of the undeniable truth—*he couldn't control the things that mattered to him.*

Pulling in a strangled breath, he approached the man. "You shouldn't be driving."

"Go-a-way-fro-me," the bearded man said, shoving him back. "I-m jus-fin."

"Sure you are," said Bliss, biting back the anger from his voice. He seized the man by the arm. "You're coming with me."

"The hell-I . . ."

Bliss dragged the man up the stairs to his loft, then through the other door down to the DAF room. Phillips's voice rang clear through the air. The music muffled the sounds of the man trying to resist his iron grip.

"You're going to stay here and sleep it off." He tightened his hold on the man's arm. "Do you understand?"

The man's eyes were half-closed, on the verge of passing out. Bliss shook him. He released the man when he sagged against the wall. Then he stormed over to one of the cots and opened it. He retrieved the man and deposited him on it. None too gently. The man was out cold.

Bliss stomped down the hall, not caring that he stank, was covered in dried sweat, sporting five-finger running shoes, or that he was bare-chested. Someone was going to answer for this. He had rules in this bar, and people would follow them or get out.

He paused at the mouth of the hallway, surveying the crowd. His eyes locked on Phillips strumming away on his guitar up on stage. *What the hell is he doing up there? He isn't supposed to sing until next week.* His jaw clenched. It was insubordination. WTF wasn't Phillips's stomping ground when he wanted his ego stroked. There were reasons for a schedule—better staffing and having a bouncer to deal with such a crowd. Fisting his hands at his sides, he pivoted and walked to the bar. He would deal with Phillips later. First, the drunk in the back.

River and Sarah were buzzing back and forth behind the bar. Both looked tired yet moved effectively around their half of the bar. A sliver of his anger was clipped away. He stopped two feet from River and shot her a menacing stare. He was sure she would freeze at his brooding look. He counted the seconds. It was a no-go. She didn't even flinch.

Her lean, well-curved body moved with a grace it didn't have two weeks ago. She was in the "zone" of serving, which was good and bad.

After a minute, his irritation had run over. He pointed to a customer. "What do you want?" he ground out, knowing the only way to talk to River and Sarah was to lighten the workload.

"Four Bud Lights."

"What table?"

"Right corner, back. Five of us."

"Do you have a DD?" he asked, recognizing the man as

the loadmaster of Hovercraft Fifty-Four.

"Yes. It's Rogers."

He went to the fridge and grabbed the man's drinks. River bumped into his side and jerked around to see what she'd run into. The crease in her brow was deep. When she recognized him, her face softened. His heart hitched. A face of stone, he turned away from her and handed the loadmaster his beers.

"Do you have a tab running?"

"No, but can I start one?"

He looked him over. The loadmaster did have a DD. "Sure, but I'll be watching you guys."

"As if I would expect anything else, Chief." The loadmaster pressed one of his beers to his forehead, saluted Bliss, and shimmied back to his group.

"Smart ass," Bliss murmured to himself.

He pointed to another man who claimed the loadmaster's spot. "What are you having?"

Bliss took over the corner of the bar, and River moved over to work the middle. He noticed her carefully avoiding Sarah's space, but she held her ground when Sarah rammed into her several times. He could see Sarah was testing her. How far would Sarah go to outshine River? He groaned inwardly. It was never good when Sarah saw someone as a threat or a challenge. He knew firsthand how determined she could become.

Thirty minutes passed, and he was still salty and shirtless. That didn't matter, however, to the women who were infiltrating his corner of the bar. Finally, the crowd on the bar thinned, and he could talk to River and Sarah. Things had slowed down. Phillips was taking a break and had come to stand beside him. Bliss ignored him.

"Sarah, River, DAF room now." He turned to Phillips. "You work the bar for a few minutes while I have a chat with these two."

"Sure. Do I get a free beer?" Phillips asked optimistically.

Bliss checked his irritation with him. He'd been friends with Phillips long enough to know why he sang tonight. He must've gotten bored waiting for Shots and him to show up for their pool and darts playoff tonight.

"Okay. One beer. Stay out of the hard liquor."

Phillips's face scrunched up, and he threw his hands into the air. "What? Me? Never."

"You heard me, Tinker Bell. One beer."

"Fine." Phillips crossed his arms over his chest and pouted.

"Seriously, you're a grown man," Bliss complained with a touch of disgust in his voice. "Have some self-respect and act like one."

Phillips shouldered past him and then leaned against the counter, smiling at a cute brunette who just muscled in past two displeased gentlemen—debating the merits of the 49ers versus the Cowboys—to place an order with him.

Bliss marched back to the DAF room with River and Sarah in tow. On his way, with every step he took, images of the news reporting on the accident a mere few weeks ago played in his mind. His body grew heavy with the weight of that day, and the grief he carried.

He hardened his heart and entered the DAF room. He was ready for any outcome.

River didn't know what the problem was, but it couldn't be good. Her thoughts snagged on Bliss calling Phillips "Tinker Bell." She couldn't focus on Bliss or Sarah. A slow-moving joy crept up from her toes. Tinker Bell was Phillips. Mathew had talked about him and how he was always there for him. And Bliss knew of the nickname. One of the pieces River didn't know about Mathew's life fell into place.

Bliss stopped just inside the DAF room. Sarah brushed

past him. River was confused. Watching him storm into the bar with a grumpy face, striding in like an angry lion, his fierce-looking muscles rippling in his shoulders and back. His clipped movements said it all. Her anxiety rose as the seconds stretched out.

Bliss flipped on the lights and River's eyes widened. The man with the peppered beard was passed out on a cot. Her heart fell. How did he get to the DAF room? It wasn't Sarah. She'd been working the bar with her all night. She'd seen the man in the corner of the bar before she'd gone to the restroom an hour ago. She began to pick at her shirt. He must have left.

For a few seconds, Bliss didn't speak. Then he glared at River and Sarah with such intensity. Before she could say a word, Sarah took up residence beside him, hip pitched out to the side, arms across her chest, and her perfect blonde hair framing her face. River knew she was going down. Here was Sarah's moment to even the score.

"He's not mine."

"Did you serve this man alcohol?" he asked River.

She felt like a trapped lizard ready to break off her tail to try to escape. "Yes. He was here when Chrissie turned over the shift."

"Did she tell you to keep an eye on him?"

She fisted her hands in her shirt. "Yes."

"But you didn't, did you? Even after what I told you." Sarah looked at her with disgust. "You're so stupid. I knew she would mess up. Can you fire her please so I can go back to work?"

"He had his four drinks then got up from where I was working. I didn't know he was still inside until I took a bathroom break. He was at a table with some other guys."

"And you didn't go and check on him to see if someone else was getting him drinks?"

Sarah was in her face now, and River felt her temper flare.

She wasn't taking any crap from this woman.

"Get out of my space," she said through gritted teeth, shoving Sarah's shoulders.

Bliss pulled her back. "That's enough, Sarah. I'm the one handling this." He was calm, but there was a deadly hardness in his tone. "Do you know where I found him?"

Her eyes flicked from Sarah to him. It took a minute for his words to penetrate her anger at Sarah. "Outside," she could only whisper.

"Yes, I found him trying to get into his Ranger. Do you know what could have happened if I hadn't seen him?"

Tears burned her eyes, but she blinked them away. "I was going to check on him after I went to the restroom, but when I came back, there was a crowd at the bar waiting for drinks. I got distracted," she forced out, her chest aching.

"That's not good enough," Sarah complained. "You have to know what's going on in the entire place, even the patio."

A knot formed in her throat. All she could do was stare at Sarah.

"Sarah, did you tell her about the drink rule?"

"Yes."

River watched him fist his hands, and his brows drew down. She could see he was struggling with what to do. He needed her because of Rose leaving, but the magnitude of the situation weighed heavy on him.

She was going to have to fight for this. If she wanted it. She focused on Bliss, heart pounding in her ears. She searched his face for . . . she wasn't sure what—hope, perhaps, for a future she didn't want to admit she'd been dreaming of.

She didn't find it. His eyes were piercing, ablaze with fury.

"I am sorry. I understand why you would be upset." A pain squeezed her heart as she thought of Mathew. No one knew better than her what devastation a drunk driver could bring about. "I won't let it happen again. I can do better."

"It's not a question of doing better. It's the fact that you didn't act on your instinct to check on him." He frowned.

"I had to go to the bathroom. I got distracted with customers."

Sarah smirked, entirely too pleased with his retort. River shook off her instinctive fear. She stepped up to him. Her face was barely a few inches from his.

"Fire me then and get it over with," she said, poking him in the chest as hard as she could.

He didn't move, but she watched his pupils expand. His hard expression remained. She recalled the day she'd interviewed and the desperation she'd heard in Rose's voice. She saw the calculation in his eyes. Could he pick up enough of the slack if he fired her and avoid stressing Chrissie and Sarah? She wanted to see how badly he needed her. Not as a warm body to hold tightly against his, but as a valued employee of his bar.

"I want you to leave," he said finally.

Sarah squealed with joy. "Oh, it's about time—"

"I didn't serve him more than I was allowed." That was a stretch and she knew it. But technically, it wasn't a lie. She served the other young man. "When he was sitting at the bar, he had seemed fine. Go ask Phillips. He was talking to the guy before he slipped away to the other side of the room." She reached around Bliss to poke a finger into Sarah shoulder. "If anyone should be asked to leave or get into trouble, it should be her. She's the acting manager. She should be watching over me, helping me. Not just being an Evil Barbie."

He stepped away from River. She hadn't backed down from him or from Sarah. He hadn't gotten to her. That in itself was a victory worth celebrating in her own time.

"Go home. You're suspended for three days. Think about what happened tonight and how you won't let it happen again."

"What?" Sarah cried, grabbing his arm.

"I'll see you on Monday," he continued, shaking Sarah off.

"But, Bliss—"

"Shut it. Go check on Phillips."

Sarah narrowed her blue eyes, tossed her golden hair, and marched out of the DAF room.

She was speechless for a moment, but then she found her voice. "Thank you for not firing me." Her eyes filled with the gratitude she felt.

"Don't," he said, turning away from her. "Don't think for a second that I did this for you."

He walked over to the stairs that led to his loft from the DAF room. She didn't know why those few words cut so deep. She knew it wasn't because of their . . . indiscretion. How could it be? It didn't, however, take the sting away. A terrible regret assailed her, and anguish stabbed her heart.

Her chin quivered, but somehow she was able to pull herself together. "Whatever the reason, thank you."

She rushed out of the room to collect her purse and left the bar before he saw her cry.

CHAPTER NINETEEN

Pool balls smacked together as smoke from the patio drifted in. Shots tapped Bliss on the shoulder. "You okay?"

Bliss was irritated and distracted. He ignored his friend and leaned over the pool table to take his shot.

"What the hell's got you in such a bad mood?"

Bliss tipped his head back and one-eyed him. "I caught a guy trying to get into his truck after we got back from running."

"How is that a bad thing?"

"He was drunk." His scowl was hard and deep.

"It's a bar."

"It's my bar," he yelled. "You know what can happen." His face was a picture of torment.

Shots took a step back. It was as though Bliss had struck him across his face. Shots looked at the ground. Everyone in the bar turned to look at Bliss who slammed his fist on the table.

"I won't be responsible for another death. I won't, even if she hates me."

"Who will hate you?"

"River."

Shots seemed at a loss for words. "You want to call it a night?"

"No." Bliss flopped back down into his chair. "I won't be

able to sleep with her running through my head . . ."

Shots smirked. "What did you do, Bliss?" He seemed impressed that Bliss had claimed River. "I didn't know if you had it in you to claim anyone. I thought Logston would win her over with his charms."

"She was supposed to watch him. She said he left the bar, but she saw him later in the corner with some other guys but did nothing. I had to suspend her," Bliss said.

"For how long?"

"Three days."

"Could have been worse. You could have fired her."

"I wanted to. But Rose would kill me. I can manage for a few days without River."

Bliss had wanted to stop her, to tell her he was sorry. But the thought of Mathew and the man who had killed him made his blood run cold. That would never happen again. Not at his bar. If suspending River caused her to despise him, it was a price he would pay a thousand times over to keep the community safe. He tried to erase the hurt he'd seen in River's eyes. He did care for her, but there was just no room for a relationship.

Logston flopped down into the chair next to Bliss. "Safe to assume I shouldn't give him sharp objects? Say a dart to finish this game with Phillips?"

Shots laughed as the cue ball smacked the two ball hard into the right corner pocket.

"Fifty says he's mad enough to throw the dart at you," Phillips chimed in. "Come on, he's the best. I bet he can nail Logston in the chest from across the room."

"I don't feel like getting stabbed for your entertainment." Logston glared at Phillips.

Bliss leaned back in his seat, his head low. "I'm not throwing darts at anyone, not even Logston."

There was silence for a moment. Then Shots snapped his

fingers. "Why don't we go watch the security footage so you can really see what happened? Then you'll know exactly how bad you should beat yourself up."

His head snapped up. "What?"

"Come on, Bliss, get it together. Remember these things called cameras." Logston pointed to the corners of the bar toward the roof.

"I forgot about those. All I do is clear them once a month, and most of the time Rose does it."

Bliss was on his feet and rushing into the DAF room before Shots had even pushed out his chair. He was furious with himself for not thinking about the security footage before he confronted Sarah and River. He swiftly unlocked the small door hidden beneath the stairs that led to his loft and peered inside. Only a single chair fit in the room and one small table with a monitor on it. He pulled out the chair and sat down. Footsteps were heard from behind. He glanced back and nodded to Shots, who leaned over to see the monitor.

He brought up the security footage and backtracked for a few seconds, not sure how fast and how far back he should go. He stopped the footage and checked the date at the bottom of the screen. The screen flashed several seconds of different scenes from the five cameras scattered around WTF.

"Damn, over two weeks ago." But when he looked up, his stomach turned to knots. He pushed play and saw Rose pressed up against the wall, desperately twisting against Chapman to break free of his hold.

"I'm going to kill him," Shots said, slamming a fist against the wall.

A rustling came from the DAF room and then a loud snore. Bliss cursed. He'd forgotten about the man with the beard. It was obvious River was more than a distraction; she was a nuclear bomb that had been dropped into his life.

He watched the screen helplessly as his sister was assaulted. Chapman leaned into Rose, pressing hard on her belly. He clicked on the volume of the monitor. Rose's cries filled the small room. "Chapman, stop! You're hurting me. You're hurting the baby. Please stop."

Chapman laughed. "Why should I? You don't love me and I don't love you. I know the baby isn't mine. I know it's his."

He grabbed Rose by the neck, still able to keep her hands in place.

Rose choked and gasped for air. "Please . . . the baby."

Shots pounded his other fist into the wall. "Fuck."

Bliss knew about the bruises on Rose's wrists, but the choking? This was his proof. Rose couldn't keep quiet any longer. She was going to have talk to someone.

The screen flashed to another area of the bar. He skipped the footage forward. He watched the date change in the corner of the screen. He didn't know why, but he stopped on the day River had walked Rose up to the loft. It had been a few days after they'd locked Chapman in the container. He watched the scene change. He found what he was looking for, but had hoped not to find.

"Shots, look."

Chapman's car was parked outside. Rose pulled in and got out of her car when Chapman climbed out and ran up behind her. He began to drag her toward his vehicle.

Bliss shot to his feet and slammed his head into the low ceiling, and dropped to the seat once more. "Holy shit, he's stalking her," he said, holding the top of his head. "Why the hell didn't she said anything to us?"

Shots was red and growling loudly. "He's not stalking her. He was retaliating against us. She doesn't know what we did. And this is probably why she hasn't said anything because we would either make it worse or we would end up in jail."

He scrubbed a hand over his face. There had to be something he could do that Rose wouldn't kill him for. The footage. He would take it to the police and get a restraining order on Chapman to keep him away from the bar. He might not be able to get Rose to do it for herself, but he could find a way to keep her at the loft. Then if Chapman got close to WTF, he would have him arrested. He took great satisfaction in knowing he now had proof of what Chapman had been doing to Rose all along. But what did Chapmen mean by the baby wasn't his? Bliss shook it off.

Now to see what really happened today with River.

CHAPTER TWENTY

River drove around town for hours, not wanting to go home. She still couldn't believe she hadn't been fired. She knew Rose had been her saving grace, knowing how much Bliss loved her. He wouldn't do anything to get her upset, which reminded her . . . River pulled over to the side of the road and rummaged through her purse for the piece of paper Rose had written her address on the other day when she'd invited her to come over and have coffee. She hadn't taken Rose up on the offer, but she did think it was a good idea to check on her. And she didn't feel like being alone.

She punched the address into her GPS and found Rose's apartment. But before her knuckles rapped against the door, Rose waddled out with a small bag, shoving it into River's arms.

"Thank God. You couldn't have better timing. My water just broke. I was going to drive myself to the hospital, but you're here now. Which car's yours?" she asked, eyeing the parking lot.

"The smart car," River said.

"You have got to be kidding. How's all of this . . ."—Rose gestured to her belly— "going to fit in there?"

River smiled weakly. "I can push the seat back."

She rolled her eyes and started walking.

"What about Bliss or Sarah or Chrissie or Shots or Logston or Phillips? Anybody but me. You don't want me helping you." Her heart rate increase so fast she began to feel light-headed. Rose needed her. How could she say no to Rose on this very important moment?

She gripped Rose's bag and rushed in front of her, not sure how to help other than making things easier. She opened the door, reached under the seat, pulled a latch, and the seat slid back about six inches. Next, she shoved Rose's bag behind the driver's seat and stepped away. She held Rose's arm as she climbed in with a heavy groan.

Once Rose was tucked inside, she slammed the door, ran to the other side, and jumped in. "Where to?"

"Pendleton Hospital," Rose said, breathless.

"On the base? They won't let me inside."

"They'll let you in, just go. I have a military ID because of Bliss."

"Have you called anyone?" she asked.

"I tried Bliss. His phone goes straight to voicemail."

"Right. Okay. Let's go." She prayed she remembered how to get there from her little outing with Logston. Pulling in a breath, she whipped her little car around, tires squealing, and off they went.

River cast a glance at Rose every few seconds to gauge her discomfort. Rose had one hand on her stomach, but it seemed all of her extremities were tense and pressing hard against anything they came into contact with. She continued to moan, the sound low and deep. River was horrified. *Oh shit, oh shit.* She'd never seen someone in labor other than in movies. A troubling thought emerged. What if Rose had the baby in the car, right there next to her? She eyed Rose's stomach. *Please stay in there, little guy.* She pressed her foot on the gas and drove faster.

With every groan that erupted from Rose's mouth, River's

anxiety climbed to a nine-point-nine. She shouldn't be doing this. She would go the wrong way or not get there soon enough. She was going to make Rose suffer more than she had to.

A wave of nausea hit her. Why was she getting so worked up? It didn't make sense. She tried to sort through her feelings. *Pull yourself together, you idiot,* she chastised herself. *Now is not the time for an emotional crisis.*

Rose's face was etched with pain. One hand clutched her seat and the other was braced against the window. River recalled the day of her interview and how Rose had sobbed in front of her. Compassion filled her. Rose was her friend. She almost forgot what that felt like. Too long she'd shut herself off from the world. Hiding in her office, reading about wonderful things she would never experience because she was scared. How had she let what happen in college cause her to become this person?

Tears pooled in her eyes. Why had she done that? She rummaged through the mental garbage she had carried with her every day for years. She reached for the dark hidden space in the back of her mind. All at once, her rampaging emotions halted in their tracks. As she poured light into the dark space, memory tumbled out.

She understood now. She didn't believe she was worthy . . . of anything. Not kindness, love, or even friendship because she was ashamed of what had happened to her. That she should have been smarter than to walk alone at night on campus. And because that had happened, everything her mother had ever said to her rooted far deeper than she'd ever thought possible.

She kept a death-grip on the steering wheel as she stared out the windshield. She could see now that it wasn't people she was afraid of; she was afraid of allowing people to see her inadequacy. All these years and she'd blamed herself. What a waste of time! *What a waste of energy! It wasn't her fault, none of it was.*

As she glanced at Rose, she felt something inside her burst free. She wanted to have friends. She wanted to have a relationship with Bliss. She had shut people out for too long. Tears slid down her warm cheeks.

Rose let out a wail, snapping River into the moment. There had to be something she could do to reduce Rose's stress. "Do you want to listen to some music?" She reached for the radio knob, but Rose slapped her hand away.

"NNNOOO," Rose ground out. "Just talk."

"About what?" she asked.

"Anything." Rose relaxed. Her arm slid down from the window to her lap, and her breathing slowed.

She went with the first thing that popped into her head. "Bliss suspended me from the bar tonight for three days."

"What?" Rose cried. Her brows stitched together and she scowled. "Why?"

River swore she saw Rose's nostrils flare. *Why did I say that?*

"It was my fault. I think I served a man too much alcohol indirectly. He caught him trying to get into his car," she rushed out, wanting to defend Bliss, and then she wrinkled her nose. *What is wrong with me? Why am I defending him? Because he did the right thing. He always does the right thing. That's why I admire him. It's why I like him.*

Her thoughts head-butted each other.

Rose didn't say anything for several seconds, and the weight of the silence sat heavily on her chest. She took the Camp Pendleton exit and drove up to a soldier who was standing at the gate. The fog was heavy in the air she could hardly see him.

"How can I help you?"

Rose pulled out her military ID and leaned across River as best she could.

"I'm in labor. I have to get to the hospital."

"I need to see registration and insurance."

"You've got to be kidding," Rose said, exasperated.

"It's okay. I have them right here, sir." She reached into her glove box. Rose sat back and stared out the window.

A contraction and a pissed-off cursing Rose convinced the solider to let them pass, pointing River in the right direction.

"I'm going to kill him," Rose yelled as River passed the new NEX, hurrying down the dark, lonely road.

The fog eased a bit. She could at least see a quarter mile in front of her. Her grip on the steering wheel relaxed.

"I said it wasn't his fault. The guy had been at the bar, in my area. I was watching him, making sure I didn't break the rule. But then he left . . . or so I thought. Before I took a break to go to the restroom, I saw him in the corner. I made a note to check on him when I returned to the bar, but when I came out, customers were waiting . . ."

"It's not your fault. You're new, and he has issues." Rose leaned forward and groaned loud, long, and deep.

Finally, the hospital loomed in front of them. She had never been so relieved in her life. She zipped into the closest parking spot, turned off the engine, and rushed over to help Rose.

While helping to carry some of Rose's weight and get them up the stairs into the hospital, she pulled out her cell from her back pocket. She hit the speed dial button Logston had so kindly programmed into her phone just the other night. It was almost nine p.m. She prayed he would answer. She didn't have anyone else's number. Three rings and a deep voice answered.

"Oh, thank god," she said.

"Who is this?"

"It's River."

"How's it going, sweet cheeks? I miss you. I came to see you and heard you got suspended."

"Yes, I'm sorry, Logston. Is Bliss there?"

"Give me the phone. I'm going to kill him. Tell that brother of mine I called him three times," Rose said, trying to snatch the phone from her hand.

"Was that Rose? Why is she with you?"

"Because she's in labor, and her water broke."

"Oh shit."

"Yeah, that's what I'm saying. Can you please tell Bliss to come?"

She didn't know why, but Logston went quiet all of a sudden.

"Okay, I'll let him know."

The phone went dead.

Rose made it up the stairs without a contraction and into the hospital. She was checked in and off to a room twenty minutes later.

⁓⁓

"Looks like Rose is in labor. Bliss, you better get over to the hospital. Rose will never forgive you if you miss the baby's birth," Logston said, poking a head into the DAF room.

The color drained out of Bliss. "What? Why didn't she call me?" He pulled out his phone from his jeans and saw his phone was off and he didn't even know it. *Damn it.* Rose was in labor and she couldn't even reach him. Some brother he was.

"It was River. She's with Rose. I knew she would call me if she got in trouble. Put my number in her phone yesterday."

He stiffened when he heard River's name and pushed to his feet. He wanted to tell Logston that she was off limits, but after today, he wasn't sure she was. He pivoted toward the door. Shots followed.

He glanced over his shoulder at his friend. Shots's anxiety twisted vividly on his face. Sarah stopped wiping the table she was cleaning. "Where are you two going, and why aren't you taking the other two with you?" Sarah complained.

Shots eyed her. "Rose is in the hospital."

He watched excitement spread across Sarah's face. He knew she was a pain in the butt, but Sarah loved Rose.

"Tell her I'll be there tomorrow."

He gave a nod, then he and Shots were gone.

CHAPTER TWENTY-ONE

River was perched on the edge of the chair in a corner of Rose's labor room. She grimaced and tried to stop herself from cringing. Rose's contractions caused her stomach to visibly shrink two to three inches. Her groans had lost its defiance and were now pain-filled and sad.

River couldn't sit there and just watch. She gathered her courage and rose on shaky legs to stand beside the bed. Rose's body was covered in sweat, and her white-blonde hair stuck to her face. Rose was a very strong woman, but right here, right now, there was only pain and fear in her eyes. River hurried into the bathroom across the room, grabbed a small towel, and ran it under cold water. She dabbed Rose's forehead with the cool towel.

"I never thought it would be like this." Rose's amber eyes filled with tears, and her chin quivered. "I'm sorry for crying."

"Don't be sorry." She squeezed Rose's hand. "Everything will be okay."

Rose took her hands and squeezed. "Thank you for helping me. I know you didn't have to."

The sincerity in Rose's voice caused her to abruptly tear up as well. "I'm glad I was there when you needed help."

Rose released her hands and started taking deep breaths. Another contraction.

"I want Bliss, I want Shots," Rose cried. Tears rolled down her flushed cheeks.

"I know you do. They'll be here soon." She glanced at her watch, and just then, a nurse cruised in.

"I'm going to check you and see how you're doing, okay?" The nurse walked over and gently rubbed Rose's arm. She pressed a button on the monitor and the beeping stopped.

"I'll be right back," River said to Rose, and quickly left the room wanting to give her some privacy.

She paced down the white sterile hall. *Deep breath in, deep breath out. No, wait, hold it, hold it in.* The smell of the cleaning products was getting to her, or maybe she felt awful for failing miserably at being the supportive friend Rose needed her to be.

She heard Rose cry out in pain. She fidgeted with her sweatshirt jacket, the zipper, the strings in the hood, anything to combat the helplessness growing inside her. Then he appeared. All the tension in her body evaporated.

"How is she?" Shots asked, wearing a scowl that would frighten small children. "Where is she?" He glanced around, trying to find Rose's room. Bliss beside him.

She pointed to the right of the hall. "She's doing well. A nurse is in there. You should wait until the nurse is done."

Bliss devoured her with his eyes and she almost cowered under his scrutiny. He walked toward Rose's room when the nurse hurried out. "How long do we have until the little guy gets here?" he asked the nurse.

"Could be hours. First-timers can take quite a while. She's at six centimeters now. Three to go."

"Thank you," he said before entering the room.

Shots looked awkwardly at River. "Sorry to hear about what happened at the bar earlier tonight. Try and not think too harshly of Bliss. He has reasons for what he did."

She gave Shots a weak smile, which he returned. He

stared at the door to Rose's room, as if he didn't know what to do. She smiled and gave him a shove with her elbow.

"She was asking for you. She wants you in there."

"Really?" he said, looking hopeful.

Shots slowly made his way to Rose's room. He paused before he entered. She couldn't believe it. He was scared.

Knocking lightly on the doorframe, he announced his arrival to Rose.

"Shots," Rose replied in a wispy voice.

She knew she was watching something very beautiful. The worry lines around his mouth disappeared, replaced by one of his most handsome smiles. Watching the scene play out gave her warm and mushy feelings. Down the hall, nurses chatted and checked on patients. The entire level was focused on labor and delivery. The floor inundated her with sounds she'd rather not be a part of. Tugging at her hood strings, she didn't know what to do next. Rose had all the support she needed to get her through her labor and was doing well. She didn't have to stay. It would be awkward with Bliss here. She decided to leave, but first she wanted to wish Rose luck.

"I just wanted to say goodbye before I left," River said in the doorway.

Bliss was leaning against the wall with his arms across his chest. He was glaring at Shots, who sat next to Rose.

"Stay. Please. Stay," Rose said, desperation in her tone. Rose glanced at Shots and then at her brother. There was clearly tension between Shots and Bliss, and it was obvious that Rose didn't know what to do.

She pulled in a breath and stepped into the room. She strolled past Bliss and came up to Rose. "If that's what you want, I will. I don't know if I can be of much help, and I can't promise I won't pass out when the baby comes, but I'll stay."

Five hours had passed, and River felt every second of it. Every breath, every groan, every hissing, every agonizing cry Rose let out pushed her further and further away from ever wanting to have kids. She was exhausted, and she wasn't even the one having the baby.

"I have to push," Rose screamed at the nurses holding her legs.

"Not yet. The doctor will be here in a second."

"Fuck the doctor. The baby is coming out," Rose bellowed.

River hugged her corner, trying to make herself as small as possible and avoid being involved in the carnage that was happening in the room. It was like a car wreck. She didn't want to look, but she couldn't tear her eyes away. Shots stood next to Rose and was wiping her hair out of her face. He looked excited and proud.

"You got this, Rose. I'm so proud of you. You're doing a great job. I can see the little guy's head." Shots suddenly got choked up, and so did Rose.

Next thing she knew, she was crying. She looked over and caught Bliss staring at her. But why? He should be watching Rose, not her. Something flickered over his face, but she wasn't sure what.

Three pushes later, the room was filled with the sound of a squealing baby boy. A nurse put the little guy on some sort of warming table. Shots, her, and Bliss hurried over to the newcomer as the doctor delivered the placenta and cleaned Rose up. A nurse started rubbing the little one down, a bit rougher than she thought an infant should be rubbed. The little guy was covered in—she gagged—white slime.

How could a baby be so cute and disgusting at the same time? The worst was over. The little guy stopped crying as the nurse bundled him up and placed him in his tired mother's arms. Rose was glowing. She cooed at her son, as did Bliss and Shots.

River took in the scene before her. Two grown men cooing over a baby. It was the most precious thing she'd ever seen. Her heart ached with longing.

"Well, you did it, sis. I'm an uncle." Bliss couldn't have sounded more proud.

CHAPTER TWENTY-TWO

B liss was an uncle. His sister was a mother. There was still wonder left in the world it seemed.

Shots gazed at Rose as if she was his lifeline. And for the first time, he felt sorry for Shots because he knew how it felt to want something you couldn't have.

River hurried over to Rose. "Would it be okay if I hold him before I go?"

"Of course," Rose said, happily handing her bundle of joy to River.

"Thank you," she whispered, starting to sway from side to side. Bliss and Shots watched. Within a minute, the little guy was falling asleep in her arms.

Bliss peered at Shots, who was now sitting on the bed with Rose. He gave him a "what the fuck" look, and Shots shrugged, slowly sliding off the bed and into the chair next to it.

"I can't believe it took so long for him to come out," Rose said, sounding very tired.

"I thought you were going to have him in my car the way you sounded. Had to stop myself from having a panic attack." She laughed softly.

Bliss rubbed his chest, trying to ease the growing ache. He couldn't take his eyes off River. She cooed at the baby and she looked completely in love with the little guy. He went back to studying River. She was relaxed, a natural. She was meant to be a mother. An image filled his mind. Her holding a baby . . . their baby. The idea intrigued him on so many levels. He surprised himself with the thought.

"Earth to Bliss. Anyone in there?" Shots said.

He growled in reply. The image vanished. "What?"

"As I was saying to River here—"

His nostrils flared. "You confessed your love for my sister." He didn't mean to sound so harsh, but there had always been a strict no-hooking-up-with-my-sister rule that Shots clearly wanted to break or with his suspicions already had.

Shots's eyes widened, but only for a second. He was quick to recover from being called out. Bliss was letting him know that he had his eye on him.

Shots didn't say another word. He didn't look at Bliss, clearly irritated.

He walked over to River to look at his nephew. Pulling down the blanket, he saw round little cheeks and full pouting lips.

"Isn't he cute? Rose did a great job. What is she going to name him?"

"Maddox Owen Bliss," Shots replied, still not looking at them.

"How lovely. It's a wonderful name," River said.

Bliss was overwhelmed with love for his sister. She hadn't told him what she was going to name the baby. It irked him that Shots knew. Shots was hanging out with Rose more than he let on. Owen was Shots's first name. This also confirmed his suspicions that Rose had feelings for Shots. But now was not the time to protest or make threats for breaking the rules. Shots was going to deploy soon.

He ran a finger over his nephew's soft, round cheek. He was perfect. Just like his mother. He would treasure the days

Rose would spend with him before walking out of his life and moving to Oregon. The little face tugged at his heart-strings, as did the woman holding him.

River glanced hesitatingly at him, and then transferred his nephew to his arms. "I have to go."

She touched his hand and then rushed out of the room. He couldn't let her leave. He had to fix things between them. Then he paused. What the hell was he thinking, wanting to explain? He didn't have to explain anything. They weren't in a relationship. Sure, they had shared a touch here and there and a few kisses. That was all they had and could ever have . . . right?

But the way she looked at him—truly looked at him—all he wanted to do was explain everything. What was so wrong with having a relationship? A few months ago—shit, a few days ago—he could have listed twenty reasons not to be in a relationship. But now he couldn't just let her walk away and not see her for three days. The voice in his head reminded him what and who he was: a navy chief, managing mayhem daily with a deployment on the horizon. He only had a few months left, and he was shipping out for nine months. What woman in her right mind would want to take that on?

He stomped over to Shots and gently handed his nephew over to him. Shots smiled ear to ear.

"You going to confess your love to her?"

Bliss fisted his hands and growled at his friend. He had that one coming. He quickly left the room. River was waiting at the elevator.

"Would you like to get a cup of coffee with me before you leave?" he asked.

She blinked at him, surprised. "It has been a long day. I really need to get home."

He clenched his jaw. "River, for what it's worth—"

The elevator dinged, and the doors slid open. Two women

in scrubs looked at them.

"I have to go." River stepped inside the elevator. He reached out and grabbed her hand.

"Hey now, you let her be. You either get in or you let go," said the nurse in the purple scrubs.

He closed his eyes and processed what he was feeling. Desperation. Resignation. He couldn't control people. All he could do was manage things to the best of his ability. He opened his eyes.

"Just a moment please," he said to the nurses.

River wore a tormented, confused expression. He had a bad feeling that he was never going to see her again, that this was his moment to take hold of a dream he didn't know he desperately wanted.

He had seen the security footage and knew River hadn't served the man at the bar more than the allotted drinks. But she had served the man who had been handing off his drinks to the drunk man sleeping in the DAF room. The thing was, Sarah had also done the same; she'd served drinks to a woman who was in cahoots with the drunken man. Soon, he would have to suspend Sarah as well.

"About six weeks ago, a man left WTF—he was drunk. It had been a busy night. The girls had a hard time watching who had what. I did as well. The man managed to sneak past us. He made it about two blocks in his truck. It wasn't even eight o'clock and he struck another vehicle head-on. Both drivers were killed. The vehicle that had been struck by the drunk driver was my friend."

His stomach turned. That was the first time he'd talked about the accident. Hearing it from his own lips made it final and permanent. By keeping it inside, it made it less real, and maybe, somehow, he could still change it.

But there it was. Mathew was gone.

The floor gave way beneath her feet. River couldn't breathe. Her chest was being torn open. A glazed look of despair spread over his face. She took a step away and pulled free of his hold. There was no way he could be talking about Mathew. The report never said anything about where the drunk driver had come from. She shook her head in denial. She'd never dreamed he had come from WTF. It wasn't Bliss's fault Mathew was dead. Tyler Smith had made the choice to drink too much and drive, whether in WTF or in his truck. That knowledge was still a stab to the heart. She opened her mouth to say something, but nothing came out. She retreated another step. She'd heard Rose and Chrissie refer to an accident that caused his moodiness of late. But she'd never made the connection.

Please, God . . . no . . .

She tried to grab hold of her rampaging thoughts and bumped into the two women behind her. "I'm sorry," she whispered.

He shifted uncomfortably, still holding the elevator doors, keeping it open.

She swallowed hard and met his gaze. Whatever he was trying to do, she couldn't process it. She rushed forward suddenly and knocked his hand away from the door. He backed away. She slammed the close-door button. The confused look on his face caused her to hesitate, torn by conflicting emotions.

Finally, the doors closed in his face. She pressed against the elevator wall. His words played in her mind. One of his friends had died in a car accident weeks ago. She closed her eyes. *Please, God, no . . .*

The two nurses' eyes were on her. She felt them probing her face. The elevator walls were closing in on her and there was nothing she could do about it.

CHAPTER TWENTY-THREE

Mathew's room was cold. It felt empty despite his things. She lay on his bed, staring at the ceiling, willing the room to stop spinning. Her world had turned upside down—again. Her mind replayed what Bliss had told her, and she wasn't sure what to believe. What she did know was that Tyler Smith had killed her brother not Bliss. She had to believe that. The report hadn't said anything about Tyler coming from the Whiskey-Tango-Foxtrot. The police had found beer cans and a broken bottle of whiskey in his truck.

"Mathew," she cried out. "I'm so sorry." She was apologizing for anything and everything.

Bliss said he had lost a good friend. He had known Mathew. She tried to be logical, but nothing made sense. Bliss never once questioned her name. Didn't Mathew talk about her? River wasn't a common name. A wave of anger and sadness washed over her. "You didn't talk about me, Mathew? What the hell?" she said.

And when Bliss came to her brother's home and kissed her, he hadn't acted as though it was familiar to him. Just another house on another street. "No, no, no," she shouted. She refused to believe that Bliss knew her brother. It just didn't make any sense.

But Bliss's expression at the hospital rooted in her mind.

The timing worked out. Bliss had said the accident happened six weeks ago, but it was actually forty-nine days ago. Maybe he was talking about someone else. She grabbed the pillow and screamed into it. Her hot breath consumed her face. Blood rushed to her head. It felt good.

She sighed heavily. But what if Bliss did know Mathew? Could his look of pain and regret be enough for her to forgive him if he really was a responsible party in Mathew's death? She wanted it to be enough. Deep down inside, she knew she couldn't keep working at a bar that may have played a part in Mathew's death. She had a life waiting for her back in Oregon. It was time to go home.

Her decision was final.

She scooted to the side of the bed and pressed her socked feet to the floor. There was a stack of boxes in the corner. The first thing to do before she continued packing Mathew's things was to call the realtor. Grimacing, she hobbled over to the desk and pulled up the realtor's number from her website.

"Hello, this is Teresa Max speaking," the realtor answered on the first ring.

River cleared her throat. "Um . . . yes. Hi, Teresa. This is River Connelly. We met last week about selling my house."

"Just one moment."

River picked at her shirt as she heard fingers typing away.

"Oh yes, your home is off Portal Avenue. Nice area."

"Yes, it is. I'm ready to put it up for sale."

"Great. I can come by tomorrow and take pictures . . . say around ten in the morning?"

She swallowed hard around the knot in her throat. "That would be great. See you tomorrow."

"Have a great day."

River sat there holding the phone, listening to the dial tone. *I will not cower, but overcome.*

She pushed to her feet and grabbed the roll of tape from

the desk. They were just boxes, and the stuff in the house was just that . . . stuff. Mathew was gone. Keeping his things, his home, going to his favorite bar wasn't going to bring him back. She marched over to the boxes and went to work.

Two days passed and River hadn't seen or heard from Bliss or anyone from WTF. She was glad. She carried the last box of Mathew's belongings into the PODS storage container and a sense of accomplishment she hadn't experienced in a very long time filled her. She'd done the impossible. She'd come to terms with Mathew's death.

The men sent to retrieve the PODS would arrive in half an hour. She peered up at the sky. The sun cut through the coastal fog. That was the one thing she hadn't gotten used to even after being in Oceanside for over a month. She was looking forward to going home and getting back to work. Work had been her lifeline, but somehow, she had changed. She no longer felt like it was the most important thing in her life. Yes, things would be different when she went home.

She swiveled around and looked up at Mathew's house with the "For Sale" sign in the yard. Everything was done. Her bags were packed, and she was ready to leave as soon as the drivers loaded the PODS. She glanced at her watch again, running her hands over the long braid resting over her shoulder. What was she going to do with her fish friends, Patch, Sam, Thing One and Thing Two? She didn't want to leave their fishy fate to a realtor. She blew out a sigh. She would have to bring them with her. The soft aching in her chest was getting stronger as she waited, and thoughts of Bliss flickered through her mind. She had managed to stay distracted. But now that everything was done, her mind wandered.

Shots glared at him from across his desk, but Bliss didn't care. Shots could glare at him until he went cross-eyed. He wasn't going to call River and that was final.

"What's your problem?" He finally looked up from his paperwork. The inspectors for his INSURV of Craft Fifty-Four and Forty were coming tomorrow, and he still had to input two jobs. He didn't have time to deal with Shots's stare-down.

"Nothing. Only seeing what an idiot looks like."

"Yeah, and how's that going for you?" he asked, turning to his computer.

Shots leaned over his desk. "Pretty good. You should look in the mirror. Then you will see."

He clenched his jaw. Three days he'd been enduring this kind of crap and he was getting tired of it.

Logston strolled over to his cubicle and slapped some paperwork onto his desk, frowning. "Have you seen Phillips? That Tinker Bell isn't going to be so pretty if he doesn't get his damn welders out there to Craft Thirty-Five and fix the crack in the engine module. Thirty-Five can't fly tonight. The students will have to reschedule. I put the job in a week ago."

"He's on Craft Fifty-Four," Bliss said, eyes still glued to his screen.

"What the hell is he doing on Fifty-Four?"

"What I told him to do." His hard tone shut Logston up. "I have an INSURV inspection tomorrow. I'll be here all night, as well as my guys, but those two craft will pass if it's the last thing I do."

"Thirty-Five has to fly. The captain needs his flight hours. He wants to go out with the students."

That was it. He couldn't take any more. He slammed his fists on the desk. The noise thundered throughout the office. Abruptly, the office noise dropped a notch.

"You tell the captain to forget it. It's not happening. His

flight hours are the last thing I'm worrying about, and he should be thinking the same way. We have two craft in SLEP, and we have two ready for INSURV. One is in maintenance, and two are underway with the *USS Boxer* for two weeks. If the captain wants to get his hours, tell him to line the fuck up and wait for a craft, because my guys are working on my priorities, not his. Maybe if he'd stop putting hours on a craft that doesn't need it, shit would stop breaking. If he spent more time managing the unit and less time worrying about flying, we would have more craft running."

"Well, tell him how you really feel, Bliss," Shots scoffed.

Logston's eyes were wide. *Hell.* He hadn't meant to blow up at his friend, but they were all driving him crazy.

Logston walked off. Two heads popped out from behind nearby cubicles.

"Nice, Bliss. Real stinking nice," said Shots, walking off after Logston.

Bliss had pushed to his feet, ready to go after them, when his phone vibrated in his chest pocket. He pulled it out and glared at the number. *Sarah.*

"What do you want?" he bellowed into the phone.

"Save that bad mood for someone else."

He held the phone out and looked at it, clenching his jaw. He didn't have time to deal with her either. "I can't talk right now." He hung up.

"Got a problem, Teahan?" Bliss barked at the blank-faced man looking at him from across the aisle.

"No, only taking in the show. What's this, intermission?"

Bliss flipped Teahan the bird, and Teahan started laughing.

"Rough day?"

"Don't you have a pre-inspection to do?"

The phone rang again. Sarah. *Doesn't she know when to quit?*

"What?"

"I thought you'd like to know River hasn't shown up for work."

He frowned. "What do you mean? Her suspension ended yesterday."

"Well, she's not here, and I've called her. There's no answer."

"Maybe she doesn't have the schedule?"

"I know you're busy, so I'll remind you that we schedule two weeks out at a time. She knows she's supposed to be here." Sarah's voice partially purred in his ear.

The fight drained right out of him. "I can't leave. You'll have to call Chrissie."

"I can do just fine on my own. Just thought you should know."

Bliss was in a fog. He collapsed into his chair, staring at his computer screen filled with active jobs that needed to be completed. *She didn't come in.* Why wouldn't she come to work? Sure, she was probably pissed about the suspension . . . unless . . .

Acid rose to the back of his throat. He lowered his head on the desk and groaned miserably. An itching feeling crept through his veins, causing him to scratch at his arms and shift in his seat. The shifting turned to restlessness. He cursed. "You've got to be kidding me. What the fuck?"

His chest clamped tighter and tighter. He wasn't a kid. There was no way he was having an anxiety attack. He scratched his arms roughly. Red, blotchy spots were already forming. He tried to sort through his rampaging emotions. He knew he could be honest with himself . . . maybe if he tried hard enough.

What did he really want from River? He had never asked her if she planned on staying in Oceanside permanently. Why would he if he couldn't even admit to himself that he wanted to talk about it?

Okay, he wanted River. Badly. That was that. End of story.

He had to talk to her, because if he didn't, he would become a very unhappy, mean, and miserable man.

Shots came stomping back and stopped in front of his desk. "What the hell is wrong with you now? I've only been gone fifteen minutes. Let me guess. You were overcome with guilt for treating your friends like shit and you tried to scratch yourself to death."

"Fuck you," Bliss said, running his nails up his arms and down the side of his neck.

He was nothing but sunshine and rainbows today. What a mess. The more he tried to do the right thing by controlling the things around him, the worse things got.

"Sarah called." Bliss cleared his throat. "River hasn't shown up for work today."

Shots pulled out a chair. "And you didn't see this coming how?"

"She could have gotten someone killed. I could have fired her, but I didn't. The least she could do is show up for work."

"You really are an idiot."

$$\approx \mathcal{I} \subseteq$$

River had a few hours before she had to head to the airport. She glanced around the coffee shop where she was meeting Chrissie. No sign of her yet. She relaxed as she waited, inhaling the delicious smell of coffee beans. People were gathered in clusters all around the coffee shop. Her eyelids fluttered closed and she pulled the scent in.

"You know, you look a little crazy with that expression. If I didn't know better, I would think you were getting off."

River's eyes popped open and her cheeks heated.

"Come on. Let's get coffee and sit outside so I can smoke," Chrissie said with a wide smile.

"Sounds good." She got up, and together they strolled to the counter. "What do you want? My treat."

After they ordered, they waited for their drinks and suddenly River felt uncomfortable. Was she doing the right thing by leaving? She could always wait until the house sold. She'd never thought she would like California, with its warm weather and tropical plants, everyone browned from the sun all the time. She preferred trees that shot up into the sky so high she couldn't see the tops. She thought about Bliss and the connection they'd made, not just physical. There was something about him that spoke to her in a deeper way, as if he, too, held onto a deep pain. Maybe it was the pain that came with trying to do the right thing. The right thing wasn't the most popular thing these days. Integrity suited people when they wanted it to. She'd seen him stand against his friends when they wanted to do the fast and easy thing which wasn't always the right thing. She sighed. It was lonely standing against people.

"So why'd you want to meet? I know about the suspension already. I had to listen to Sarah go on and on about the whole thing." Chrissie's eyes probed River.

"I wanted to talk to you about my brother's house."

Chrissie went abnormally still. Her relaxed demeanor was gone. A blast of steam from a vat of milk caused River to go momentarily deaf. It took a minute for her to gather her thoughts and jump back into the conversation.

"I have decided to put my brother's house up for sale," River said.

They took their drinks outside. Chrissie chose a table off to the side and away from everyone else. They pulled out their chairs and sat down. Chrissie leaned back and allowed the afternoon sun to soak in for a minute.

"What does selling your brother's house have to do with me?" Chrissie asked.

"I fly out this afternoon to go back to Oregon," River said. She sipped her coffee to hide her nervousness. She had to stay focused and get through everything before she left.

"What? You better not be messing with me. Why?"

"I can't stay here any longer. My therapist thought this would help me grieve for my brother, but I just can't do it anymore. I have to go home. I have a life back there."

Chrissie appraised her for a second, then plopped her cigarettes on the table and pulled one from the pack. She lit it and took a long drag. "This is because of him, isn't it?" she asked.

"Because of who?" But River already knew Chrissie knew, but she didn't want to say his name.

"Ha-ha. I wasn't born yesterday. You and Bliss. Are you running away?"

"I'm not running away," she said defensively. She pinched the bridge of her nose. "Look, I don't want to talk about him. I just wanted to give you a set of keys to the house, if you don't mind. That way, if something happens before it sells, someone can get into it other than the real estate person."

Chrissie laughed and then shrugged at her, taking another drag from her cigarette. "Just keep telling yourself that."

Chrissie was acting odd. River ignored it and pulled out the keys, placing them in front of Chrissie. "I just wanted to let someone know that I was leaving. That's all. Will you take the keys or not?" River was shaking. Her nicely submerged emotions were trying to surface. She'd thought Chrissie was her friend, but maybe she'd been wrong.

Chrissie slowly took the keys and put them into the pocket of her shorts. "I'll check on it. I didn't mean to upset you."

"Thank you for helping." River pushed to her feet to go, but Chrissie stopped her.

"Just so you know, Bliss doesn't do one-night stands or light dating. He won't admit it, but he's a nester and just doesn't know it yet."

"Thanks for all the training. You were a great teacher, and you've been kind to me. Sorry I couldn't stay and do you proud."

"No worries. Maybe you'll come back."

She chuckled. "If you're ever in Klamath Falls, drop by." River pulled out a piece of paper with the addresses to Mathew's house in Oceanside and to her house in Oregon. When Chrissie opened the paper, her expression softened and turned sad. River was confused.

"Take care."

"You too. If you ever need someone to talk to, you can always call me."

River fixed her fake smile upon her lips and pivoted around. Before she could take another step, her stomach turned to vinegar. She'd kept silent about her brother to everyone but Chrissie. She had to ask her if she knew Mathew.

She glanced over her shoulder. There was a spark of some undefinable emotion in Chrissie's eyes as she rubbed a thumb over Mathew's address. River didn't have to ask. The answer was there on Chrissie's face. Tears rolled down Chrissie's cheeks as she folded the paper gently. She pulled out another cigarette and placed it between her lips as the tears continued to fall. After a moment, she put the paper in her front pocket.

River shared in the moment of Chrissie's grief over her brother's death. Perhaps they were friends, perhaps lovers. The thought made River's heart swell and ache all at once. Mathew could have had someone to love before he was killed. He might have been happy and in love.

She rushed back and hugged Chrissie tight before letting go of everything.

This was goodbye to Oceanside, California. Goodbye to Bliss . . . and goodbye to Mathew.

A warm breeze danced through River's hair as she stood in front of Matthew's headstone. Shame tightened every muscle. It had taken weeks to gather the courage and see where her mother had chosen to lay her brother to rest. Peering out at the harbor and the many boats skimming over the water she knew there was no better place to spend eternity. The cemetery was tidy and well kept. She sank to her knees and touched the raised letters in Mathew's name.

"I miss you so much. I should have been here sooner . . . but I just couldn't bring myself to see you in this place. To know this was your home now." Tears ran down her cheeks and fell onto the grass. How many tears had been the water that feeds this green grass?

"I met some of your friends, I think. I haven't really asked because I knew it would hurt that they knew you better than me. They are all amazing. I wish I could have seen you with them." She pushed a strand of hair behind her ear. "I put your house up for sale and boxed up most of your stuff. I hope you don't mind I got rid of some of your stuff." River puffed out a breath. "This is so dumb. It's not like you can do anything about it. I don't know what the hell I'm saying."

She picked at her dress. "I love you. I miss you. I'm sorry if I let you down. Sorry that I hid stuff from you because I thought I was protecting you. I know now it kept us from being close like we used to be. Thank you for loving me."

Running a finger over his name one last time. "You were an amazing man, Mathew, and I will take you with me always. Be good." She kissed two fingers and placed them next to his name. Her brother, forever and ever.

CHAPTER TWENTY-FOUR

By the time Bliss climbed onto his Harley to go home, it was midnight. He was exhausted. His craft would pass INSURV, he was sure of it.

As he drove off base, he left work behind him. Every thought that filled his mind was of River, and he felt as though he was on a craft riding a tide of emotion over which he had no control. She had the power to take him under as easily as she could lift him above the swells.

He missed her smile, the way she smelled like flowers, the way she fidgeted with her clothes when she was nervous, and he missed having someone to spend time with. He had to make it right.

When Bliss pulled up to River's house, his blood went cold. There were no lights on, and there was a "For Sale" sign in the yard. He parked his bike in the driveway, climbed off, and stormed up to the door and pounded on it, fear rising. It had only been a few days.

There was no answer. He pounded harder, causing the door to shake. He waited. Still no answer. He moved to the front window and tried to see past the blinds. A sliver of light shone through the darkness. Bliss squinted. The living room looked empty. Where had she gone? He stormed to another window that didn't have blinds. The kitchen was empty. Everything was empty. She was gone.

He staggered back as if struck by some invisible fist. He rushed to his bike, fired it up, and took off for WTF. When he got there, Chrissie was cleaning tables and Sarah was behind the bar. There were a few people talking and having drinks in the back booth. He clamped down on the urge to yell at Chrissie and Sarah in front of customers. He stomped over to Chrissie because she was the first to make eye contact with him.

Before he even opened his mouth, her hand flew up in front of his face. "If you're going to have some kind of attitude, I don't want to hear it. I'm not in the mood to deal with an MMI today."

He blinked, surprised by the somber look on her face. Chrissie was always in a good mood. She was one of those people who livened up a room. He wondered what could have happened to make her unhappy. Glancing at Sarah, he cast off his concern. He had his own issues to deal with at the moment.

"I wanted to check if anyone has heard from River yet," he asked in his best "I'm not going to yell at you" tone.

"Yes," she said, moving to the next table.

Crossing his arms over his chest, he waited for her to elaborate, but she didn't, and he felt the vein in his forehead start to pulse. "Where is she?" he demanded.

Chrissie looked up from her cleaning to meet his hard stare. A sudden icy contempt flashed in her eyes. "She's not here, obviously."

"I have to talk to her," he said, running his hands through his hair.

Chrissie looked away and walked to the next table. She grabbed the bottles and glasses, clanking them against one another. She put them on the tray she was carrying and swung around, detouring around him and making her way back to the bar. He popped his jaw and fisted his hands. What was her problem? Why was she acting like Sarah?

Slowly, very slowly, he followed Chrissie. *Manage. All I can do is manage. I can't control.*

"Is she coming in tomorrow?" He stood at the bar counter.

"Nope. She's not coming back at all," said Sarah, the corners of her mouth tipping up, eyes sparkling.

"What do you mean she's not coming back?" The vein in his forehead pulsed harder. Fear flooded him, as if he had taken on bad fuel. He couldn't breathe, and he rubbed his breast bone, trying to stop the painful ache. Why would she leave? She knew Rose couldn't come in and work. He'd explained why he had to suspend her when they were at the hospital. Everything should be fine. She should have understood.

Chrissie glared at Sarah and set her tray down. "She left," she said, looking irritated. "And why do you care?"

He didn't reply, merely walked over, yanked open the fridge, and pulled out a beer. He twisted the cap off and chugged it until it was empty. He slammed the bottle down on the counter. River had fled. He had driven her away with the knowledge that he failed to control his bar and someone had died from it. He thought she understood why he had gotten upset about the drunken man trying to leave the bar, but it seemed he was mistaken.

"It's better that's she gone," said Chrissie under her breath as she placed the empty glass bottles into the recycling can.

"Damn straight. We don't need her. I tried to tell you that." Sarah pitched a hip out at him. "Her breaking bottles of whiskey. Her being afraid to be around people. I don't fully understand where that one came from, but it's no concern of mine. Her letting people drink too much and leave. Why would you want that in WTF after Wagner?"

Wagner. Even the sound of his name caused him to wince. Bliss's blood pressure increased with every word she spoke.

"Why are you such a bitch to everyone? What is your problem?" Chrissie barked. "You hate yourself so much that you treat everyone else around you like shit. I can't listen to you talk about River like that. She doesn't deserve it, and Mathew would kick your ass." Chrissie threw her hand over her mouth. Tears shimmered in her eyes, and she made a break for the patio.

His brain processed her words too slowly to catch the weight of what she had said before she disappeared. What did Mathew have to do with River? And then it hit him. That smile, it had felt familiar. He hadn't been able to put a finger on it. The way she tipped her chin up at him. The heart-broken expression when he talked to her about the accident. He was seeing Wagner in River. When the weight landed on him, he felt his knees go weak.

"Mathew, River . . . Pee Wee. Mathew's sister," he whispered to himself.

Sarah didn't say anything, but she did look surprised by the news. Her mouth dropped, and for a split second, she looked sorry about what she'd said, but only for a second.

He marched out onto the patio. Chrissie leaned her butt against the railing, and a cigarette was pressed between her lips. Tears rolled down her cheeks. He'd never seen Chrissie cry before.

"Don't lie to me. Did you know who River was the whole time she was here and never told me?" Bliss couldn't stop his voice from rising.

She looked away.

"Chrissie."

"I'm not Rose. That won't work with me," she snapped.

"I'm sorry." He cleared the irritated tone from his voice and started over. "Have you known who River was?"

Chrissie wiped a tear away from her cheek, looking very pale. "No. One day we were talking. She said she was in

Oceanside because her brother had died a few weeks back. I mean, people die all the time, but something made me think she could be Mathew's sister. I started watching her more closely after that." Chrissie turned to Bliss. "I mean look at her. She looks just like him. I don't know why I didn't connect the dots sooner. Didn't you ever get the feeling she reminded you of someone?"

He couldn't deny it. He had found himself regarding River with a sense of familiarity from time to time. "Why didn't you say something to me?"

"I didn't know for sure until today when she asked me out for coffee. She told me she was leaving. She gave me Mathew's address. Then I knew." She sucked on her cigarette a few times and blew out a cloud of smoke. "Why would I tell you anyway? So we could watch you shut down from life because you feel guilty for something that wasn't even your fault?"

"What're you talking about?"

"Oh, please. I know you. What was one of the first things you thought after the accident?"

He didn't say anything.

"You felt guilty. You probably even thought, in some messed-up way, that you had killed Mathew."

He frowned and looked away from her. Apparently, she knew him very well.

"Ha . . . I knew it." She pointed at him with accusation in her eyes. Then her face softened, and she touched his arm. Suddenly, Chrissie was very serious. "Bliss, I'm not going to tell you where she is until we set a few things straight."

He appreciated her honesty and how fiercely she was protecting River.

She dragged in a rough breath and began. "You have to stop feeling responsible for the actions of those you care about. Fate touches all our lives."

A tear trickled down her cheek. His throat closed. One of the hardest things he had to endure were tears. He wanted her to stop, but he let her cry. He knew this was important to Chrissie.

He searched her face. "Did you love Mathew?"

Chrissie nodded. He never knew she cared for his friend, but it seemed to be a theme lately.

"The guilt has to stop. You never could've known that guy had alcohol in his truck, and that he had been drinking in the parking lot before he drove off. How was anyone to know that? Stop beating yourself up. Get over your control issues and learn to live again. It's okay to be happy."

She clasped his shoulders. "If we'd changed one thing—one single thing—you wouldn't have met River. She would've never come to Oceanside. She would've continued to be the workaholic Mathew said she was. Everything happens for a reason. There's always a bigger plan than what we anticipate day-to-day."

He felt a heavy weight lift off his shoulders. He had been beating himself up for weeks about many things. He dropped his head. She was right.

"I'm not sure I know how to be happy. River made me happy, and look what I did to her."

"What did you do that can't be fixed if you love her?"

"That's the problem. She doesn't know I love her."

Chrissie stepped back and looked at him. "Does this look like my surprised face?" she said, pointing at herself. "River asked to see me because she wanted someone to know where she was going. She wants to see if you'll come after her."

"Did she tell you that?"

"Not out loud, but I could see she was hesitant about leaving. Every girl wants the man she loves to go after her. Don't let her down. We women put a lot of faith in a man. Maybe that is our biggest flaw."

He sighed. It all made sense now that it was out in the open, but damn if it didn't throw him for a loop. Chrissie was right; it was time to stop holding onto the guilt he'd felt every day since the accident. He wasn't sure how long it would take him, or if he would ever fully let go, but he was willing to try for River. No, not just for River, for Rose, for Chrissie, for all the people he loved. The more he tried to hold on, to control those he love, the more they pushed him away.

"Can I have her address? I'll get her back." He allowed the emotion he felt to shine through his face. It was a good time for truths.

Chrissie studied him for a long while. He didn't like feeling so exposed and vulnerable, but he knew if he didn't show Chrissie what she wanted to see, he would never get the address.

She finished the last puff of her cigarette and smashed it out in the ashtray. Then she pulled out a paper from her shorts and placed it in his palm.

"Don't mess up again, Bliss. You don't always get a second chance."

CHAPTER TWENTY-FIVE

River adjusted her backpack and glanced at the seat number on her ticket. Her eyes flicked between the numbers above the seats, then she claimed her window seat, fastened her seatbelt, peered out the window to the runway, and sighed. She was finally going home. Closing her eyes, she waited for relief to fill her, but it didn't come. There was no relief, only emptiness. If she was honest with herself, she was sad to be leaving. Bliss had fired up some wild thoughts about the future she'd give little time to over the years. For a time, her grief had been eclipsed by an evil Barbie, a drink list, bar procedures, a pregnant manager, and a group of pestering men. She'd work through many of her anxiety triggers that stemmed from her assault. She would have liked to have one more chance to be alone with Bliss. She smiled at the thought. Even if she never saw Bliss again, she was happy for their time together.

When everyone was in their seats, the captain's voice came over the speakers. "Good afternoon, everyone. We have clear skies all the way to San Francisco. There shouldn't be any problems making connecting flights. I hope you will enjoy the flight."

She ignored the flight attendants giving their safety instructions and thought about the manuscripts waiting for her. Her boss had been kind to let her use her vacation days, but he had been ecstatic to hear she wouldn't be taking an extended leave of absence. Her phone was ringing off the hook all morning and she was forced to turn it off. There was nothing she could do to help him until she was off the plane and at home.

As they pulled away from the terminal, she closed her eyes. She wanted to go to sleep and pretend this trip had never happened, and that Mathew was only out at sea.

"We will be landing in about twenty minutes."

That was all River caught as she tried to pry her eyelids open. She rubbed the sleep away from her eyes and was surprised she'd slept through the entire trip. That was a first. She hit the attendant button. A minute later, an attendant appeared from behind her.

"How can I help you, ma'am."

"Could I please get a soda before we land?"

"Sure." A minute later, the attendant handed her the soda. "I hope Coke is okay."

"Yes, thank you."

River pressed against the window and gazed at the beautiful land that stretched out beneath her. Bliss was at work and would soon notice that she'd missed her shift. What would he do when he found out? She envisioned the vein in his forehead popping out and his lips pressed into a thin line. She giggled unexpectedly.

Poor Chrissie was probably working a double shift because of her. Would Chrissie tell Bliss she'd left, or would she keep it to herself? She frowned, not knowing the answer to that. And poor Rose. She was going to be upset and worried that the bar was short one bartender before she packed up and move to Portland, Oregon. Rose would be a few hours away and River vowed to go see her when she got settled in. That was if Shots would let her leave. River had a feeling things were going to change between them.

She bit the side of her cheek. Her timing was not ideal for

the Whiskey-Tango-Foxtrot for sure. But when she recalled the utter disappointment and disgust on Bliss's face the day she'd been suspended, she couldn't blame him. She felt ashamed that she hadn't been more attentive to the bearded man. Who knew what would have happened if he'd gotten behind the wheel of his car that night.

The landscape beneath her grew closer. Buildings sprang up all around. Cars drove on the thin lines of road. Checking the time, her heart skip a beat. She had thirty minutes to get to the next terminal and board the next plane.

The airplane's engines roared, and then the plane touched down. With a little bounce, she was back on solid ground. One more plane ride and she would be home.

She grabbed her backpack and slung it over her shoulder. Halfway down the aisle, she realized she'd been on a plane surrounded by people, and she hadn't cared in the least. When she arrived to California a few weeks ago she had been in such a state of numb grief her anxiety hadn't had a chance to take hold. But now it could have and didn't. A smile broke across her face, and then she took off in a hurry, praying she would make it to her next flight.

Finally, she was home.

River waited for gratitude to flood her being. *It didn't come.* She felt it again . . . that hollowness. As she stepped onto her front porch, she felt as if she'd been stabbed. The hurt was something she'd never experienced before. The pain suffocated her, making her want to drop to her knees. She staggered forward. The closer she came to the house, the worse the pain grew, wrapping around her body like barbed wire. Gripping the strap of her backpack, she bent and clenched her jaw, determined to work past the suffocating pain. *I will not cower, but overcome.* The phrase echoed through every chamber in her mind. Why was she cowering? And how would she overcome it? Confused, she peered up at her shelter, her sanctuary.

Slowly, she reached the front door. Her hands shook as she fumbled for her key in her pocket. She slid the key into the lock and turned it. When she pushed the door wide open, she was hit by old, stagnant air. Mail littered the floor. Hesitantly, she walked inside, stepped over the bills, and closed the door.

She'd been gone for weeks, but it felt like yesterday when she heard the news that changed her world. *Don't do this to yourself. Don't start looking back. Look forward. Think about all the work you have to do.*

As she went upstairs, she tried to keep her mind blank. She dropped her backpack onto her bed, stripped off her clothes as fast as she could, and hurried into the bathroom, turning on the shower.

As she held her hand in the water waiting for it to warm, she started to tremble. The walls of her determination crumbled. Before she fell apart, she stepped into the shower and allowed the water to rush over every inch. With every moment that passed, she felt a bit calmer and was able to breathe a little easier.

Afterward, River was dressed in her most comfy sweats. She was feeling better and could now enjoy being home. The scent of old wood filled her nose. She loved the smell of her house. It was her escape from the world. But when she opened her eyes and looked around, something felt different. The house felt empty and sad, or perhaps it was only her. A worried feeling washed over her that maybe she would always feel sad. Maybe she shouldn't have come back.

She started at herself in the mirror. She looked the same—maybe a little tired—but she was the same person. "You're fine, River," she said to herself. But she wasn't the same person and never would be.

Her fish had arrived. Never in a million years did she see herself shipping fish to herself. But here she was staring down at Patch, Sam, Thing One, and Thing Two. It was time to see if they liked their new home. She strolled past the large indoor fish tank she'd bought them for winter. It had taken her two days to dig and landscape a large pond for these little guys equipped with a waterfall like Mathew's. She set her fishy friends down next to the water. They would need a few hours to adjust to the temperature before she mixed them in with the new water. Sitting next to her fish, River thought about her neighbor and all the peaches loaded on the tree. It was time to make a friend.

CHAPTER TWENTY-SIX

For the first time in a week, River felt somewhat normal again. It surprised her how quickly she was able to adjust to being back home. The heat of the day soaked into her pores as she reached for another lovely peach. Fish splashed around in their new home.

High on the ladder, she held a laundry basket against her hip. Ever so enthusiastically, she filled the basket for her neighbor next door. The elderly woman would be surprised to see such a gift.

River worked faster, anticipating the smile on her face. Once the basket was filled to River's liking, she climbed down the ladder and out of her tree. When her bare feet touched the thick green grass, she wiggled her toes. Summer had never seemed so happy to her before.

Walking tenderly over the neighbor's stone path, she made her way up the porch steps that mirrored her own. As fast as she could, she pushed the doorbell and swung away from the door, wanting to hide the basket.

Slippers shuffled against the wooden floor and then her neighbor appeared at the screen door. "Yes. Can I help you?" asked an aged voice.

River's mouth spread into a wide grin, and she turned and presented her basket. Smiling brown eyes met her hazel ones.

"Oh my goodness. What do you have there?" the woman asked in a curious tone, peering at River's basket.

"A gift that has been long overdue. I'm River Connelly. I live next door."

"Really? Connelly." She raised a thin gray brow. "I've seen you before. Always hiding away, aren't you?"

River felt heat rush to her cheeks. "Yes, ma'am." She cleared her throat. "I brought you some peaches." She tipped the basket so that the contents could be seen.

"Thank you, Jesus. I thought I was going to have to continue stealing them." She winked and opened the door with a wrinkled hand. "I'm Mrs. Barham. Come in, have some tea with me on the back porch."

"Oh, thank you, that would be lovely. It is such a nice day for sitting," River said.

"That it is. That it is." Mrs. Barham led the way into the house. The layout was the same as River's house. The only difference was Mrs. Barham's home was filled with old, sturdy-looking furniture with knick-knacks scattered on shelves and bookcases. As she was led into the kitchen, Mrs. Barham stopped at an old maple table.

"Put the basket here, please."

River did as she was asked and placed the peaches on the table. Mrs. Barham gathered a tea pitcher and two mason jars with handles.

"Come on. Out this way."

"Can I help you with anything?"

"No, thanks. I may be old, but I'm not dead."

River smiled and tugged on her rose-colored shirt. She did her best not to fidget, but failed. On her way out to the back porch, she spotted a bookcase down a narrow hall, which led to what looked like an office. On the shelf were all the books of her favorite author, A.J. Wrath. She stopped and stared. Mrs. Barham made it out to the porch before she realized she wasn't being followed.

"What's the holdup? Something catch your interest?" Mrs. Barham asked.

Heat once more moved to River's cheeks. "Um, yes." She walked out to the porch. Mrs. Barham handed her a jar of tea.

"Have a seat."

"Thank you. I see you are a fan of A.J. Wrath."

Mrs. Barham chuckled. "I guess you could say that."

"I love her work."

"Do you now? I am fond of it myself, since A.J. Wrath is my pen name."

River's jaw dropped in disbelief. No way her favorite author lived next door. She had been editing her manuscripts for years. She must have looked dumbstruck because Mrs. Barham laughed, totally amused. It took River a few minutes to pull herself together.

Mrs. Barham sat down beside her and sipped her own jar of tea.

"Do you write?" asked Mrs. Barham.

"No, I haven't for years." River sipped her tea and gazed out into the distance. "Although the last few days, I've had dozens of story plots running through my mind. I've started brainstorming a couple. It would feel good to write them down."

"Yes. Yes, it would. Writing has been my therapy. It kept me sane when Mr. Barham gets my foot to tapping, making me impatient to deal with his nonsense."

River felt her thoughts drift off to Mathew and then to Bliss, but she was able to push them away.

Mrs. Barham gave her a probing look. "Did you like my last manuscript?"

River blinked hard. "How did you know I'm your editor?"

"Every email I get from you is signed, 'Best regards, Ms. Connelly.' That's you I am assuming."

River swallowed. "Yes. That would be me." She blushed. "I did like it, but I think something was missing. I haven't worked it out yet however."

"You come back over when you do. So, why did you bring me peaches? I know you've seen me desperately trying to reach them in the past. You know, being a thief at my age is not an easy thing."

River chuckled, and Mrs. Barham gave her a wink and a wide smile that reached her eyes. Seeing it warmed her heart. She felt as if she and Mrs. Barham had always been friends, and she knew that was not a feeling to ignore.

"I don't know . . . things are different now. I want different things in my life. And giving you such a simple gift seemed right."

"You came out of hiding for me. I'm flattered." Mrs. Barham reached across the table and patted her hand. The gesture was very sweet of her.

"Different can be good if it gets me my peaches without needing an act of God to reach the branches."

"You are welcome to come and take as many as you want any time."

"I'll do that. Thank you."

The two of them were sitting, sipping tea and enjoying the afternoon when she spotted someone pass by the fence. She sat up. There was someone in her backyard.

"Did you see that, Mrs. Barham?"

"See what, my dear?"

"There."

Just then, a frustrated growl filled the air. A growl that caused the hair on her arms to stand. "Do you mind if I use your ladder?"

"Go, go."

River hurried over to the ladder that Mrs. Barham used to reach the peach tree. Her heart hammered. She was afraid to believe—didn't dare hope.

As she climbed the rungs, she peeked over the fence, and there he was—tall, dark, and moody. Bliss shook the handle of her backdoor. Her heart tripped over itself. He was here. He swung around and raked his hands down his face, and then he collapsed on her back porch.

She pressed her lips together, silent . . . just watching him. His hard expression softened, and God, he was beautiful. She meant to yell at him—for not stopping the man who had killed her brother—but as she watched him, she could see the dark circles under his magnificent eyes and the worry lines etched around his perfect mouth. He hadn't slept in days. His eyes were luminous with all kinds of emotions she didn't dare name.

She went up another rung so her head could be seen over the fence.

"What are you doing here?" she asked.

❧

Bliss saw movement at the fence. There she was, staring at him from the other side. Was he at the wrong house?

She chewed her bottom lip as the sun gleamed off her long brunette hair. Her cheeks were pink from the sun, and his chest tore open at the sight of her. He held fast to her gaze, afraid to break the connection. *Please, baby. Please give me a chance.*

She must have seen the desperation he felt, because she moved higher up on what he was assuming was a ladder. She stopped. His heart pounded so hard surely she could hear it even from across the yard.

"What do you want? Why are you here?" she asked, louder this time.

He didn't want to do this with a fence between them, but he hadn't come all this way to turn back. The separation from River had nearly driven him to the brink of insanity.

He rose off the porch, and with determined steps, made his way to her. "I had to see you," he said, stepping squarely in front of her.

Her expression hardened, and her chin lifted.

He frowned. *Not good.*

"Why? You don't owe me anything."

It was a slap to the face. His head dropped. *All I have to do is be honest and tell her how I feel.* He lifted his head and studied her. "Yes, I do. I owe you my deepest regret for the loss of your brother. Mathew was my friend, my brother. I need to know if you can forgive me . . . so I can move forward."

Her expression faltered for a split second. *He surprised her. Good.*

"It was an accident."

"If you truly believe that, why did you leave and not tell me goodbye?"

Her chin quivered. He stopped himself from reaching for her. And it killed him. He wanted nothing more than to yank her over the fence and take her into his arms.

"River, please, can we talk somewhere else? Inside, perhaps?" he begged, hating the sound of his voice.

Suddenly, she was gone, and a round wrinkled face of a woman appeared.

"Why, hello," she said, raising her brows up and down at him. Then she yelled over her shoulder. "I'll take him if you don't want him."

A moment later, River appeared five yards away on the same side of the fence.

"You don't want him, Mrs. Barham. Believe me, I know," River said.

He didn't like the way she said that. Fear snaked around

his heart.

He waited, allowing River to control the situation. He beseeched her with his eyes, but he didn't say a word. He took in her bare feet, faded jeans, and her top, and decided that this was what heaven looked like: River Connelly.

He tried to act as if his life was not hanging on the line. He took in the yard that surrounded her home. "Your house looks great, and this is the biggest peach tree I have ever seen."

"Best tasting too," piped in the old woman.

"Thanks, Mrs. Barham, I'll take it from here," River said, flashing the woman a knockout smile.

"Okay. I'm going to get started on some jam. Thank you again. I will bring you some when I'm finished."

After the woman was gone, River came toward him. He reached out and cupped her cheek, unable to go a second longer without touching her. He rubbed her soft, warm skin with the pad of his thumb. Carefully, he gathered her into his arms and held her close.

There was no reaction, but he knew at that moment that it didn't matter if he was a chief in the navy or a bar owner. He didn't want to be anywhere else.

Her voice was a whisper. "Is that the only reason you came all this way? To ask for forgiveness?" Bliss could hear the sadness, and it knifed him in the heart.

"I came because I love you." He rested his cheek on the top of her head and pressed her tighter against his body. Her fingers gently touched his back, as her arms circled his waist.

"Oh, Bliss," she cried, burying her face against his chest. "I'm sorry I left without saying goodbye, but after the hospital, I was ashamed that I had almost allowed the same thing to happen. If that man left and had gotten in a wreck. I just . . . couldn't live with myself . . ."

He pulled back so he could see her face. The green in her

hazel eyes ate up the brown, and tears pooled in them.

"I've missed you," she said. "I thought I could come home and go back to my old workaholic life, but I couldn't. I felt trapped . . . and empty."

He pulled her closer. "I've missed you too, beautiful."

River sniffled and molded her body to his. Running her hands under his shirt, she caused his blood to hum with longing. He needed to hear her say that she loved him as well. He would wait. He would give her time. He ran his fingers through her hair. He rubbed her neck, and he heard her sigh, melting into him. He smiled to himself. There was hope.

She pulled out of his hold and stepped back. Taking her hand, he laced his fingers with hers, not wanting to break their fragile connection.

"I shouldn't have let you leave."

"I should have stayed." She shook her head, and her hair cascaded over her shoulder. He fought the urge to reach out and touch it once more.

"I can't hide from what happen to Mathew." River's eyes collected tears. "I love you, Bliss."

She loved him. He couldn't ask for anything more in his life—not even making Senior Chief or Master Chief—than those three words.

"Say it again."

He was a breath away from her now. He squeezed her fingers to encourage her.

A loving smile tipped her lips, and her eyes bloomed with hope and love. "I love you, Maddox Bliss."

That was all he needed. All his worries and fears faded with those words. He scooped her up into his arms and marched toward her back door.

"Key."

"No key, it sticks."

She gave it a pull and then a shove, and the door opened.

She swung her feet happily while in his arms, as she placed tender kisses on his neck and ear. The fire inside him roared. He forced himself to focus on the task at hand. He peered down the narrow hall and spotted the staircase he was sure led to the bedrooms. He climbed the stairs three at a time and thanked God the house was small.

CHAPTER TWENTY-SEVEN

River was gently placed on the edge of her bed while Bliss bent over her and she took his face in her hands and kissed him. She let her lips linger, savoring the taste of him. He held her snugly against his lean body as his lips explored hers.

He stripped off his shirt and tossed it to the floor. He pulled her in and kissed her, heartbreakingly slow. All the heartbreak she'd felt in her life softened, warmed, and molded together. Not perfectly, but enough to start again. She wasn't going to be afraid anymore. She wasn't going to let the past change a future she desperately wanted. When they both surfaced for air, she whispered feeling playful and buoyant, "Lie on the bed."

He raised a brow, but did as she said. Unbuttoning his pants, he kept his eye on her. She blushed. He kicked off his pants and happily threw himself on the bed. In black boxer briefs, he rolled onto his side, tugging off his socks.

God, he's handsome . . .

She clutched the hem of her fitted t-shirt. Slowly, she slid the cotton fabric inch by inch over her skin and over her head, and his eyes sharpened. He was watching her every movement. The shirt fell to the floor, and she heard his sharp intake of breath. She wore a navy blue silk bra. It had been prophetic that she chose to wear it today. It held her breasts perfectly in place. She wanted to see his face when she took it off. Her heart beat faster as she unhooked the clasp of her bra. The silk easily fell away, freeing her breasts, which bounced rather dramatically. He swallowed hard. As he stroked his erection, she was breathless for a moment. This show was affecting her as well as Bliss.

She leaned forward slightly and pushed her jeans over her hips. Her hair tumbled over her shoulder and skimmed her breasts. She gasped at how sensitive they were. Her nipples tightened and formed round little pearls peeking at Bliss from beneath her hair.

He was pushing his boxers over his narrow hips and down his powerful legs. She had caused him to grow hard. She smiled to herself.

Tucking a finger under the waistband of her matching navy blue panties, she prepared to remove them. Before she could, he rose to his knees and crawled to the edge of the bed, then gently pulled the fabric down.

Bliss gripped her hips. They gazed into each other's eyes, and he drew her closer to the edge of the bed. He trailed feather-soft kisses from her neck and down to her erect nipples. He kissed one, then the other. His tongue glided over her skin, and he started sucking. His hands explored the soft lines of her back, her waist, and her hips.

Heat and a sort of hunger rushed into River's veins, and she drew herself closer to him. She caressed the strong tendons in his back and neck. His kisses lowered to her stomach, and his hands glided down her thighs. She pulled in a breath. Her need grew hotter.

Skimming the inside of her thigh, he touched the curls guarding her most private place. He slipped a finger deep inside her, and she gasped aloud, moaning with pleasure. Bliss pulled her onto the bed and she rolled him onto his back. She wanted to taste him. She wanted him to want only her.

Bliss was eager—too eager—to take River. Her mouth was heaven. The warmth, the pressure, the idea of it all was pushing him to the edge faster than he wanted. He held on to his control by a very thin thread.

She trailed kisses over his stomach. He grazed his knuckles over her nipples and saw the hunger in her bright eyes. She was a drug he couldn't get enough of. He'd never wanted anything this badly.

As she covered his body with her own, her legs rested evenly on each side of him. She captured his lips, and together their tongues twisted and rolled. He wanted her to shudder against him with her release. To feel her body tense against him.

"Bliss," she whispered.

He rubbed against her core. She leaned back, offering herself to him. She grabbed his shoulders, digging her nails into his skin as he entered her. She was so close he could feel the coiling of her body. River moaned and then hissed. Her wet core and her walls clamped down on his shaft. He stroked her deeply until she became breathless. Her core gripped his shaft. He moved faster, harder. Together release gridded their bodies. He moaned her name, filling her, claiming her as his own.

She melted against him. He cradled her in his arms. With her hair hanging loose, her eyes closed tight, and her bottom lip pulled in by her teeth, he decided ecstasy looked good on her.

He needed her in more ways than just this. He wanted her to stay by his side always. He ran a finger up and down her spine, his mind drifting over the past few weeks. His life had never felt so out of control. Mathew's death, Rose-Shots-Chapman, the bar, and work. Everything seemed to shift him off his axis. He couldn't help but wonder if that was what had to happen to prepare him for this strong stubborn woman to walk into his life. She nuzzled his chest and a lost piece of his heart clicked into place. He tightened his hold on her never wanting to let go, but he needed to do something—something he'd been thinking about since River arrived in his office and tipped her chin up at him. In defiance or challenge he hadn't been sure, but he'd never been so intrigued in his life to get to know a woman and go against every rule or vow he'd put in place regarding relationships. Now here he was in love with one of his best friend's sister.

He pressed his lips. He thought about Rose and Shots. He was going to have to cut them some slack. Whether Wagner was here or not he was breaking a rule. He smiled to himself. Wagner would kick his ass if he knew what he was about to do. He would have gotten in Bliss's face, maybe even shoved him back a step or two. They would have stood toe to toe. Bliss would have been scared Mathew wouldn't accepted that he loved River and wanted to make her happy. Mathew would have peered into Bliss's soul. Would have cursed him out and then wrapped him in a bear hug. The image was so strong Bliss couldn't breathe and wiped a tear from his eye. He was certain Wagner would be pleased looking down from the heavens to know River would be looked after by someone he loved. He shimmied off the bed and stared at his pant pocket.

"Did you love my brother, Bliss? Were you his close friend?" River ran a finger down his back and kissed a trail to his neck. Every touch set a fire beneath his skin. He fought the urge to pull her beneath him and devour her. He focused on her words.

"Yes. He was a glue I couldn't rub off." His chest rumbled a chuckle building inside him. "When we first met, Mathew's enthusiastic nature made me pause. He was so eager to learn about the hovercraft and what we did at the unit. I couldn't help but get caught up in his eagerness. Our first deployment together, he unloaded his hummer on to the beach and instead of going off with his unit he came and sat with Logston, Shots, and me. He asked hundreds of questions. We told stories, we laughed, and I saw in his eyes the day he decided we would be friends. It was the day he told me about you. His Pee Wee. He trusted me with concerns and some of his pain."

Wet tears glide down his back and knew River was crying. He turned and rubbed a thumb over her cheek, kissing them away. So much regret, concern, and hope turned inside him. He just wanted to hold River in his arms. "I'm sorry I didn't know you were Mathew's Pee Wee. Him and all his nicknames. Your brother knew how to keep things fun and entertaining."

She closed her beautiful eyes. "Yes, he did."

Bliss let her go. "I should have known you would come to take care of everything. I don't know why the guys and I assumed it would be your mother." He ran a hand over his face. "All those stories about you being a workaholic. Working as an editor. The way you lift your chin. It screamed Mathew all over it. I was so blind."

River kissed his neck and whispered into his ear. "Its okay. We are okay. Things will be different now. Things will be better. You can talk to me about anything. I will listen."

Bliss blew out a breath and bent down, rummaged through his jean pocket for a second, and then he stood holding out a hand to River.

"What?" She eyed him suspiciously.

He smiled his best smile and took her hand as she reached for him. He led her into the bathroom and turned on the shower.

"Seriously, what're you doing?"

"What does it look like?" he said, hopping into the shower first, allowing the cold water to cool his blood. He was rarely nervous about things, but with River he found himself vibrating at an eight constantly. It was irritating because it was proof he couldn't control everything. So he managed the mayhem that were his emotions. Desire flared in her eyes as her gaze roamed over his body. He adjusted the temperature of the water and then tugged her in.

"Really? A shower?" She pressed her perfect round breasts against him. A wave of nerves washed over him, but he pulled in a breath. He'd come here for a reason, and he was one to see things through even if it cost him everything.

He claimed River's full lips with a hungry kiss. Then he wrapped his arms around her and gently slipped a ring on her finger.

Her face was confused and she lifted her hand. Her mouth dropped, and her eyes searched his, questioning. She must've found the answer because she started dancing around in the shower. It was the sexiest thing he'd ever seen. He smiled, feeling like his life had just begun.

River was so surprised she didn't know what to do. Happiness seeped into her every pore as she stared at the gold band and the three diamonds, the center one sitting higher and larger than the two beside it. It was a traditional engagement ring. It was perfect. She busted out her happy dance, a dance she hadn't done since she was a kid. And it felt good, really good. She knew what the ring meant, but she very much wanted to hear him ask.

"Thanks, it's beautiful."

She started to pull the ring off her finger but he stopped her. "It stays there."

"But . . ." She tried to put on her serious face, but it was difficult with him looking so vulnerable. She decided to help him out. "It's only a ring until you say something." She ran her fingers over his wide chest. Water rushed over his skin and down her arms. She flushed with desire.

He raised a brow and rested his hand over hers. "I'll keep you forever . . . if you let me."

Her heart pounded as loud as a gelding's hooves against the ground. Inside, she melted. It was not a traditional proposal, yet somehow it was perfect coming from him. She pushed to her tippy-toes and brushed her lips against his.

"Forever is a long time. I don't know if you can handle all of this." She captured his lips with hers. He eagerly accepted what she gave. Their tongues rolled and sparred together. His hands skimmed over the sensitive skin of her breasts. He kissed the tops of them and then her neck until she was breathless once again.

Then he whispered in her ear, "The courthouse closes in an hour."

It took her a minute to process what Bliss was saying.

"Courthouse? What? Why?"

He was smiling handsomely at her. She melted a little more. She memorized him just like this—that smile that made her world feel whole. She wanted to see him smile all the time. He handed her a bar of soap. Then it clicked.

"Wait . . . you want to get married now?"

"Yesterday, if I could have." He chuckled and caressed her cheek. "That's if it's okay with you."

She rubbed soap over his chest and shoulders. He kissed her nose and took the soap from her hands and began rubbing her body with it. There was hunger in his eyes. She couldn't have been more pleased. He soaped her faster, shaking his head. What had been a lonely, heartsick day had turned into something extraordinary, and it wasn't even over yet. She was alive, and she was going to live—really live—as Mathew had always wanted her to.

"Yes. Let's do it."

Bliss pulled her against him, and she wrapped her arms around his neck. "Let's go then."

River loved it when he got bossy, but she would never admit to it. It would be her undoing. She kissed him, slow and long.

He reached behind her, turned off the water, and lifted her off her feet. She wrapped her legs around his waist and deepened the kiss. Bliss carried her out of the shower. Dripping wet, she clung to him. Every touch, every movement he made, stoked her need of him. The thought of having this man in her life every day, waking up in the morning with him beside her, and falling asleep in his arms every night, overloaded her senses. Her kiss grew more passionate. Bliss moved faster, and the next thing she knew, she was gently placed upon her bed. Bliss groaned and broke their connection. River protested.

He glanced at his watch. "Maybe tomorrow would be better."

She blushed. Then he was there, pressed against her, hard and ready. She gazed into his amber eyes. "I love you."

Bliss pressed his forehead to hers. "I love you, too."

Then he made love to her. Taking her higher than ever before.

ABOUT THE AUTHOR

R.E.S. Tidmore has been writing fiction for fourteen years. Ever since she was a young girl, she has always had a vivid imagination and a knack for telling stories. Now, she's able to put her stories to the page.

Connect with R.E.S. Tidmore

Follow her on Facebook: R.E.S Tidmore | Facebook
Visit her website: http://restidmore.com

Note
Visit my site and read more extras on the series you love to keep the story going until the next book. Also please help me reach new readers by writing a review of this book at the retailer you purchased it from. Your support is the greatest asset a writer could have. Thank you.